Spiritwarrior

THE COLEMANS' LEGACY BOOK 2

JAMIE BEGLEY

Young Ink Press Publication
YoungInkPress.com

Edited by CD Editing
& Diamond in the Rough Editing
Cover Art by Cover Couture

Connect with Jamie,
Facebook.com/AuthorJamieBegley
Instagram.com/authorjamiebegley
JamieBegley.net

Preface

Their names were forgotten, erased from existence, becoming just another Native American couple torn from their native land. The woman carried in her womb the gifts given by the gods, in repayment for defending the Mother of Creation. The gifts were to be bestowed on their children and the future generations to come.

As their days grew dark with their struggles to survive along the perilous journey to their new homeland, the gods watched their courage, yet never once did they try to take advantage of the stone the man carried within his chest to lessen their hardships.

Decades later, they were buried side by side on the land they had worked tirelessly on to leave a lasting legacy to their children. The secret had been sworn on and died with them, and the threat to humanity lost for all time. Mankind would never know of how close they had come to extinction, nor of the sacrifices made by the man and woman who died protecting the secret.

Fate was given the duty to watch over their children, carefully monitoring how the gifts were used by the couple's progeny. As new generations were born, Fate came to Mother in concern that their gifts made other humans fearful of them and were seeking to destroy what could not be understood in the human realm. Mother began watching them herself to see what consequences the gifts had wrought, making adjustments when needed. She might have created Earth, but it was still a work in progress.

From Hades, they had been given the gift to create and manipulate fire and to astral project themselves through the Shadow realm of time. Wisely, Mother had deemed this gift too powerful for one mortal to hold, splitting the gift into two. One to be given the power of light, the other of the shadow realm, capable of walking between Earth and Heaven. Both must be born at the same time, for light must keep darkness from consuming the shadow realm.

When their progeny nearly died out from disease, Mother called on Zephyrus to bestow his gift of wind on a descendent. Fire cannot breathe without air.

Rocque, the Lord of the Forests, had been given the gift of controlling nature. Mother watched those who welded that power closely, as the gift almost rivaled her own power over Earth. Jealous, she decided to finetune that gift, limiting the recipients of that particular power of Earth, only allowing them to wield it within their own domain, and able to shelter and protect those they love within the boundaries of the mountain they called home.

When one unexpected gift came to light, Mother could only shake her head. Her son, Poseidon, had snuck the power of water on the woman, as a reward for protecting the stone. Water can give life or take it away with a fury that could mimic her own when she was angry.

Shaking her head in amusement at some of the progenies' misdeeds, Mother didn't let her growing affection for the family sway their punishment when Asclepius' gift was misused by one of the female descendants, by saving a life meant to be taken. Sadly, Mother had Fate intervene to break the family line in two different directions. The repercussion was severe in which any of the descendants gifted with the healing arts were separated from the main trunk of gifts, which were becoming more powerful each generation.

While she didn't regret separating the family into two branches, she felt sorrow witnessing the cruel hardships the new branch had to endure. Wanting to prevent such a harsh punishment in the future, she gave them her last gift.

She had taken Astraios' gifts away as punishment for fighting with Chronos. Mother bestowed his powers which she had carefully hoarded to herself, giving the progenies the ability to read the stars and the skies, allowing them to read the paths laid out for them to follow. It was a huge gift, which would come with severe penalties if they misused it.

To make sure no family member overstepped their boundaries again, she decided there would be a safeguard born into each generation, which would have the ability to harness all the powers gifted to them. They would be her failsafe. They would carry their knowledge and the cost of their powers to the next generation. They would teach and prepare those who would follow in their footsteps. Lessons which would warn them from abusing their gifts. Their powers were gifts and weren't to be profited from and never, ever to seek to try to usurp Her power again.

Continuing to monitor the family intermittently, despite having given Fate the duty, she watched both branches of the family grow in numbers until one particular soul was born.

A male child with all the gifts.

Mother wasn't ashamed to admit she grew fond of the mortal, yet despite her fondness, she wasn't able to change the future laid out before him in the stars. He would never find his soul mate during the lifetime he had been born into. The star-crossed lovers kept missing each other, their love destined for another lifetime.

Used to philandering males, Mother watched in amusement as her favored one didn't let a lack of a soul mate deter him from finding another way to share the love he was capable of by creating life after life. He even extended his love to an outsider. Loving each child with a pure heart, he taught his children the power of their gifts with a reference she hadn't felt in eons.

When he begot a female child that had a healing power, she cried just as hard as her father when he read the stars, showing her future. The child would become too powerful to allow to remain in their branch of the family. Not only had she been born with a healing gift bequeathed from a god, also inheriting the healing touch from their native ancestors which only one other could brag about, but like all mothers, she couldn't leave well enough alone, making the soul stronger by being able to use energy derived from nature to restore her strength.

The soul needed to be switched to the other branch of the family, where they had learned the cost of using their gifts unwisely.

Her affection for the family held her hand at removing the female child until her father was given a chance to beget the child who would one day step into his shoes.

Then, with an aching heart, she called them both to Heaven together. However, they weren't together long before the female soul was sent back to Earth. Mother made certain this time that the gifted soul would be protected by a fierce warrior and a mother who loved and appreciated the nature around her. Just as important, she would be guided by a family member who would teach her how to use the gift, tempered by the personal costs she would ultimately pay throughout her lifetime.

Mother watched the offspring left on Earth with a careful eye, seeing the same qualities and commitments to those they loved as the ancestors who had fought for her in her greatest time of need.

Finally, her patience and planning were about to come to fruition. The eight brothers had the powers of demigods, the stars were aligned to where she needed them and, crucial to her plans, they had the strength of will and courage to protect the *rewards* she was about to give them. The culmination of her plan hinged on their ability to convince their *rewards* to love them.

Love was the only variable out of her control. They would have to earn the love on their own without her help or Valentine's gift.

Yes, it was frustrating for her ... So many variables could go wrong ... She had made so many promises. Mankind's fate was on the line yet again—there was a battle looming on the horizon, and those eight demigods were the only way to bring order back to the mortal, and the immortal realm. She was now at the hardest part of being Mother. All she could do was watch and trust her demigods prove their valance. It would hurt her deeply if they failed, because she was at an impasse. She couldn't interfere, despite all her immense power, held in the palm of her hand. It all hinged on the most basic of human emotions ...

Love.

Prologue

They were the first settlers. The woman, heavy with child, was unable to go on with the others who had been driven from their homeland. Her husband, determined to save his wife from their merciless demands, had snuck them away from the military officers to escape through the heavy wilderness.

Once they were out of sight, he had tugged her up the mountain, and they had made it halfway to the top when, auspiciously, they had found themselves in a clearing, having just enough time to make a hasty shelter before their son was born. The husband held his son in his arms as both of them listened to mounted soldiers starting up the mountain in pursuit. The frightened snorting of the animals indicated they were being spooked away.

It was only near dawn, after hours had passed in silence, did they venture to speak.

"What should we name him?" she asked, attempting to put on a brave face.

The father thought of the lone military officer who had taken pity on his wife's condition and had made sure she was never whipped liked the others, who had given them part of his rations so they weren't forced to either eat tainted rations or starve, and who had slipped him money from his own pocket before turning a blind eye to let them slip away after telling them there was a trading post nearby in the valley, between the sky-high mountains.

"Calian."

The woman's lips trembled in a smile. "Warrior of life," she stated. "He will have to be to make it out here."

"We all will have to be. It will not be easy," he warned.

A small laugh escaped her as she laid her head back down wearily. "To give her credit, she did warn us."

"Yes, she did," he said grimly. "When you are strong enough for me to leave you alone, I will go find the trading post. Officer Coleman gave me enough money to buy supplies."

"Will they sell to you?"

"He also gave me papers and some of his clothes."

"What kind of papers?"

"Identification papers. Jace told me he could get more for himself when he returned home."

"What is your new name?"

"Jace Coleman."

"So, we are Colemans now?"

"Yes."

"Calian Coleman," she said softly, staring at the child snuggled against his father's chest. "I like the sound of it. Are we going to stay here or find somewhere else to settle?" she asked, looking around the forest surrounding them.

"We are staying." His steely tone disclosed his determination.

"What if this land belongs to someone?"

"This mountain is mine."

She shook her head at him. "You cannot claim a

mountain."

"Watch me. I claimed you, did I not?"

"I am not exactly a mountain."

"Look around. Before I am done, I am going to own as far as you can see, and then some. No one will ever be able to drag us away again."

She believed him, as he never said anything he did not mean.

Reaching out, she took her son back into her arms. "I have been gifted a son and a mountain in one day." Taking the little fingers in her hand, she stared down into the sleepy gaze blinking up at her.

She pulled the infant closer as she shivered in fear. Would they be able to protect their child from the hardships ahead of them? Other than a fire and what items her husband had managed to accumulate and keep hidden in anticipation of their escape, they had nothing. Even the shelter was just a horse blanket tied between two trees.

Seeing her shiver, her husband lay down next to her to share his warmth.

"It is starting to snow," she whispered, not wanting to wake her sleeping son.

"As soon as it is light, I will build a place to keep us warm —there are enough broken limbs I can use. I will not go to the trading post until you and the baby are safe enough to be left alone for a day."

As the bright moon shone down on them, the worry and fear she had been feeling since their journey had begun inexplicitly ebbed away.

"We'll be safe while you are gone—the mountain will protect us." She didn't know how she knew that, yet she did. "That is why the horses would not let them follow us. Mother wanted us to find this place. She wanted to make sure we would survive."

Chapter One

"I'm sorry for your loss."

Sophie stared dispassionately at the lawyer as he expressed his condolences.

"I'm sure your father's death has come as a shock."

Not really, she thought sarcastically. The only surprise to her was that Marty hadn't been killed years ago.

"Law enforcement believe your father's murder was meant to serve as a message to his accomplices."

Of that, Sophie had no doubt. Marty had had a habit of surrounding himself with other crooks.

"Mr. Keates, let me save us both some time. I stopped caring about Marty when I was four years old and had to run to a neighbor's house to call for help after he nearly beat my mother to death. The happiest day of my life was when she left him. If you called me in here to make arrangements for his body, he can rot in the morgue, as far as I'm concerned."

Mr. Keates seemed at a loss for words

Sophie reached for her purse. "If that's all, I'll let you get back to more important work. I'm going to take my mother to a celebratory lunch and tell her the happy news."

"No—" Mr. Keates cleared his throat, reaching for an envelope on his desk. "I mean, there is another matter to discuss. Your father left you this letter, and there is the matter of what he left you in his will."

She didn't reach for the letter. "I don't want a dime of his money, and you can put that letter in the shredder for me."

Mr. Keates cleared his throat again. "There wasn't any money. Mr. Meyer left you a restaurant."

Son of a bitch knew she wouldn't easily throw away a restaurant. The only trait she shared with her father was their love of restaurants.

Owning her own restaurant would be a dream come true. She had been saving money since graduating high school to achieve her goal and was still thousands of dollars away from reaching it.

Her eyes fell to her lap, where she was clenching her purse. "What kind of restaurant?"

Mr. Keates looked down at a folder on his desk. "The restaurant used to be a diner before Mr. Meyer purchased it. When he owned it, he only sold hamburgers and fries."

Figures. The only meal she could ever remember him making her was hamburgers and fries.

Twisting the strap of her purse, she wanted to refuse the restaurant just as easily as she had any money. Only she couldn't get the words to come out of her mouth.

She wanted a restaurant so badly. How many years would it take to earn enough money before she could purchase one on her own?

"Where's the restaurant located?"

"Treepoint, Kentucky."

When had Marty moved to Kentucky? The last time her mother had hired a detective to find him, he had been living in Tennessee. Where in the hell was Treepoint, anyway?

Ignoring the lawyer's presence, she took out her cell phone and Googled Treepoint.

The town was small, really small. Would she even be able to make a living there?

"As I stated, there is no money that comes with your inheritance, but the business could present a good investment for you, or you could sell the property. Of course, you don't have to decide what you want to do right now—think it over." Mr. Keates picked up a thick yellow envelope, sliding the letter Marty had left her inside before he closed it and handed it to her.

Sophie stared at the envelope for a full minute before shaking her head.

The lawyer kept holding the envelope mid-air. "I understand, from your reaction to Mr. Meyer's death, that you were estranged from your father. In my line of work, I've seen family members have to deal with their emotions toward the deceased and their inheritance before. Normally, they take the inheritance as payback for the hurt they feel they had to endure from the deceased. There have also been a few, like yourself, who refuse to take anything.

"My best advice to you is not to cut off your nose to spite your face. Mr. Meyers is dead. He's not going to know if you accepted the inheritance or not. Your opportunity to pay him back for the way he treated your mother is gone. The only one who will be hurt will be you if you refuse. I don't know your financial situation"—Mr. Keates' gaze lowered to skim over the clothes she was wearing then returned to her eyes—"but I want you to think of your future instead of dwelling on the past before you make your decision." He was right, much as she hated to admit it. She hated Marty so much she wanted to award the person who killed him a medal.

How many restraining orders had her mother taken out over the years since she found the courage to leave him? Her mother and stepfather had lived in fear that Marty would find them and one of his unscrupulous contacts would kill them. It was only when they constantly moved and Karter had gone no contact with his relatives that they had found a measure of peace.

At the thought of her mother and what she had gone through over the years, she reconsidered accepting the restaurant. Her mother's health wasn't the best, yet she was working every day at a job she hated just to keep a roof over her and Karter's heads. Karter worked as well, but their constant moving had limited their job choices.

Resigning herself to the fact that she was going to accept her inheritance if she was ever going to further herself to get to the point where she could make a big difference in her parents' lives, she reached out and took the envelope.

Mr. Keates' sympathy shone out of his eyes. "It might not seem like it now, but you made the right decision."

Sophie stared at the envelope. Then why did she feel like she had just sold her soul?

"While I do think you made the right decision, I want to give you a warning. The police found out while investigating your father's death that he was involved in a counterfeit ring in Kentucky, spanning to Ohio, perhaps even further to other states. The investigation is ongoing. Perhaps it would be safer for you to sell the business rather than moving to Treepoint."

"You think the police will be investigating *me*?" Sophie gave the lawyer an unconcerned look. "Let them. I haven't seen my father since I was eleven years old."

"I'm not worried about the police. I'm more concerned, and so is the Sheriff in Treepoint, that if your father did have accomplices, they may assume you know where the counterfeit money came from."

"I don't."

"I don't believe you do," he hastily assured her. "I just

want to make you aware of the situation while you make your decision to keep or sell the restaurant."

Holding the envelope, Sophie rose to her feet. "I appreciate the warning. I'll make sure to keep that in mind. Thank you."

"You're welcome." He smiled. "If I can be of any further assistance, please let me know."

"I will."

She left the lawyer's office and made her way to the parking lot while calling her mom to make sure she was home before driving to her parents' house.

As she pulled in in front of their rental home, she saw her stepfather's car was there also.

After knocking on the door, she waited patiently for it to be opened. Then, after she gave her mother the hand signal in the camera that it was safe, her mother opened the door with a beaming smile.

"I thought you were working this morning?" her mother said, pulling her close for a hug.

"I don't go in until two. I need to talk with you."

"About what?" Her mother gave her a concerned glance as they sat down on the plain green couch.

"Yesterday, I received a letter from Marty's lawyer."

Her mother tensed, and Karter, who was stepping into the living room from the bedroom, stopped in his tracks, his face paling.

"Marty knows we're in Arizona?"

"He must have, or the lawyer wouldn't have been able to find me."

Karter moved further into the living room to sit down on a chair facing the couch and buried his face in his hands in dejection.

"We don't have enough money to move. We're barely scraping by as it is. What are we going to do?"

"We don't have to worry about Marty anymore."

Karter raised his head. "Obviously, we do, if he mailed a letter to you."

"Marty didn't mail the letter to me—a lawyer did. I went to the lawyer's office today. Marty's dead."

Her mother started sobbing, while Karter jerked to his feet to go back into the bedroom, closing the door behind him.

Sophie knew why Karter had left—her stepfather didn't want her to witness the same reaction her mother was having.

Sliding over the couch cushions, Sophie placed an arm over her mother's shoulders. "He's dead, Mom. You and Karter don't have to be afraid anymore."

"Are you sure he's dead? This could be another of his tricks."

"He's dead. I called the police department in Treepoint on the way here and talked to the sheriff. He is dead."

Her mother cried harder. "Thank God," she mumbled as she started rocking herself back and forth.

"It's over, Mom. Marty can't torment us anymore."

"Thank you, God."

Karter returned to sit down next to her mother on her other side, pulling her into his arms.

"It's finally over," she sobbed into his chest.

Sophie left them to go into the kitchen and found a full pot of coffee. She wanted to leave them so they could be by themselves but needed to discuss what else she had learned.

When she went back into the living room with three cups of steaming coffee, she told them, "That's not all."

Her parents turned their heads in her direction.

"He left a restaurant to me."

"The one in Tennessee?"

"No, this one is in Treepoint, Kentucky."

"Treepoint, Kentucky?"

"Yes."

"What are you going to do with it?"

Sophie debated telling her the whole truth about what Mr. Keates had told her then decided against doing so. Her mother would argue for her to sell it before she could go and check it out. She didn't want to make the decision until she saw the restaurant.

"Nothing yet."

"Then what are you going to do?" Her mother wiped her tears away with the palms of her hands.

"I'm going to Treepoint."

Chapter Two

J ody watched the numbers slowly flick over on the gas
pump. The turn-of-the-century pump was slow as shit.
It would be worth the twenty-minute drive to another
gas station just to save his fucking time.

A car pulling up on the other side of the pump caught his
attention.

"Fuck," he swore under his breath, seeing the woman get
out of the BMW.

"Hey, Jody."

"Hey, Baylin," he repeated her greeting cordially. "How
have you been?"

"Been better. I had to pull a double shift at the hospital,"
she responded, taking off her gas cap. She looked him over as
she walked to the side of the pump. "How have you been
doing?"

"Can't complain."

"You must be busy. I can't remember the last time you
stopped by. I haven't even seen you around town."

"Don't come much. Ginny and Alanna take care of the
shopping. Silas takes care of the rest."

"I heard Matthew got married. Tell him I said congratulations."

"I will."

Hearing the click that the gas tank was full, he pulled out the nozzle and hung it back on the pump. "Good to see you, Baylin," he told her.

Sliding up to his side, she pressed her breasts against his arm. "If you're not doing anything tonight, why don't you stop by for a while before you head back home?"

"Not tonight." Taking a step back, he felt his dick growing thick. "It's been a long day."

She ran the tip of her tongue over her bottom lip and a hand over his bicep. "Baby, I'll do all the work; you won't have to do a thing." Suggestively, she sidled closer to him. "It's been a while since I've had a taste of your dick. I'm thirsty."

His dick thickened. He was horny as hell, and Baylin always made good on her sexual promises. Why not?

You know why, Jody told himself. While Baylin could provide him the temporary release he needed, the regret would last longer.

Silas had been apprehensive for the last couple of weeks since Ezra had told him he was having trouble reading the stars. When Jody had started paying more attention, he had also noticed the change, but he himself only grew more concerned when Silas admitted experiencing difficulty.

Fynn had started spending more time outside, reading the stars, but was only able to tell them the heavens were showing that a change was coming. Silas was taking it as a warning, while his other brothers had seen it as a good sign that one of them would find their soul mate.

Since they hadn't been able to get a good read on the stars, Silas wanted them to remain on the mountain unless they were out on a job. The mountain they lived on heightened their powers while at the same protecting them from outsiders.

"Come on, Jody." Baylin slid around to the front of his body, pressing hers against his. A sulky pout formed on her lips as she rubbed her breasts across his chest and thrust her groin against his. "Baby, I can feel how hard you are for me. Why go home and waste it when I'm begging you to let me do it for you?"

His willpower shrank at the closeness of Baylin's voluptuous body. "I guess I could stop by, but I can't stay long," he told her, caving to his body's demands.

With a delighted grin, she broke away. "Let me pump my gas, and we can go."

"Let me." Directing her to stand by the door of her car, he pulled out his card before taking out the nozzle out.

The whole time he pumped the gas, he reconsidered what he was about to do. Then, when he was finished, he walked to the door of Baylin's car, which she was leaning against.

"Baylin ..."

In his mind, he had decided to tell her he wouldn't be going to her apartment. She must have seen from his expression he was going to backtrack.

"You aren't changing your mind, are you?" she asked plaintively. Grabbing his hand, she pressed it to her crotch. The thin pants let him feel she was already wet. "You don't want to leave a girl hanging, do you?"

He rubbed her pussy, then reluctantly removed his hand, horny enough to fuck her against the side of her car, regardless of the customers going in and out of the gas station's convenience store.

"Let's go," he growled thickly.

Baylin hastily got in her car.

The whole way to her apartment, he castigated himself for

giving in to his blue balls instead of going home like he had promised Silas.

Despite how much he told himself not to, he found himself parking next to her. Baylin got out of her vehicle and was waiting for him to do the same.

"Dammit." Cursing at himself, he got out of his truck to loop an arm around her neck as they went inside her apartment building.

"For a second, I thought you were going to go bail on me."

Jody pushed the button for the elevator. "I should have."

"What made you change your mind?" she asked as they stepped inside the elevator.

Jody pushed the button for her floor as the doors closed. "You're not the only one who's thirsty."

Since they were the only ones in the elevator, Jody didn't stop her from kissing him. Not holding back on her fuck-me kiss, his hands went to her hips to lift her higher to his mouth. Baylin's legs went around his waist just as the elevator door opened.

He carried Baylin out of the elevator and strode down the hallway from memory.

"Where's your key?" he mumbled against her lips, releasing a groan when she didn't stop kissing him.

She twisted her hips to reach into her back pocket for the keys. "Here."

Bracing her against the wall, he opened the door as she wiggled her pussy against his abdomen. He fit the key in the lock, then turned the doorknob.

"Hurry up, Jody!" Baylin whined, her mouth moving to his neck.

When he felt her bite his neck, he felt his cock swell harder in his jeans.

Needing to get inside her apartment before he burst, Jody carried her inside.

"Baby, you want to fuck or suck first?"

Jody winced at her loud voice. He had forgotten how loud she could be when she was aroused.

Holding her steady, he used his foot to slam the door. Then, striding through her apartment, he carried her to the bedroom and lowered her to the bed. "We can do whichever you prefer."

Baylin got to her knees and started unzipping his jeans.

Grabbing the headboard when she slid his cock in her mouth, he remembered something else about the short time they had been together.

She wasn't shy about going after what she wanted.

Chapter Three

Rolling over in the dark, Jody caught sight of the alarm clock on the nightstand. Groaning, he rolled back over to slide his arm around Baylin's waist. "I have to go."

"Don't go yet. It's not even daylight," she protested. Baylin snuggled against him, throwing a feminine leg over his.

"By the time I take a shower, drive home, and make myself breakfast, it will be." It was much easier to deny her sultry invitation after spending numerous hours in a sexual haze.

"You could be late," she suggested. "What does it matter? What's the use of being one of the business owners if you can't enjoy being late when you want to be?"

"I might be one of the owners of my family's business, but that doesn't mean I'm not responsible for my share of the work."

"One of your brothers can take over for you. They don't have a problem asking you to work when they want time off."

Jody didn't like the resentful tone Baylin used when she spoke about his brothers. Too late, he remembered why he had stopped hooking up with women—Baylin in particular.

Last year, when they had met up a few times to scratch each other's itch, she had started asking to go out on dates. He had gently told her that he didn't date. When she had pressured him the last time—her wanting him to meet her parents —he had stopped coming by. The way she was talking as if she was familiar with his family was a bad omen that Baylin was assuming more than the situational fuck session they had shared.

"You're always putting your brothers over me," she complained.

What the fuck? She just had to ruin the good time he was having.

Jody blamed himself; he knew before he had fucked her that the pleasure didn't outweigh the negatives.

"I need to get that shower."

"Come on, Jody ..." She slid her hand down his chest to his cock. "Call one of your brothers," she coaxed. Her caressing his cock didn't tempt him to make the call. "It's untelling how long before you come off that mountain again."

Not anytime soon, if he could help it.

Removing her hand, he slid out from under her legs and went to the bathroom to take a short shower. All he wanted to do was get away from Baylin. She had to have a screw loose for her to say he was putting his brothers over her. How was he putting his brothers over her? She acted as if he had never stopped coming around, that they had been in an ongoing relationship.

He toweled his body dry and walked out of the bedroom with the towel wrapped around his hips, giving an inward groan at seeing Baylin had pulled on leggings and was putting on a black workout top.

"I'm hungry," she stated, seeing he was watching her. "I thought we could grab breakfast on your way home."

He was about to refuse but felt bad when she sent him a pleading look.

"You were going to fix yourself breakfast, anyway," she cajoled. "Eating breakfast out will be quicker."

"There's no one open this early for breakfast."

Baylin's face broke into a smile. "The diner reopened. I saw it when I drove by yesterday. I just checked on my phone, and it opened at six. We can eat breakfast, and then you can go to work, and I can go to the gym."

He wanted to kick his own ass at Baylin's instant comeback.

As he was getting dressed, he thought it over. He knew he wouldn't be seeing Baylin anymore from the way she was acting. He could tell her here or put a stop to it at the diner. From the angry glimmer in her eyes, it was safe to assume he wouldn't be walking out that door without a huge argument. The restaurant was a safer bet—Baylin wouldn't want it getting out around town that his interest in her was in her imagination.

"Sure, we can do that. You ready?"

"I am." She grabbed a black jacket and put it on.

Leaving her bedroom, he grabbed his truck keys from the kitchen counter. In the parking lot, he waited until she was in her car then followed her to the diner.

From the outside, the diner looked the same way as it always had since he was a kid. Getting out of the truck, he opened Baylin's car door for her. When she would have taken his hand as they walked to the diner, he shoved his into his pocket.

Opening the door for her, he let Baylin go in first. As they stared around the empty restaurant, he saw a woman, who had her back to them, making coffee then turn around.

"Have a seat. Take any table you want," she greeted them warmly.

His mind on the coming confrontation with Baylin, he didn't pay attention to the waitress, more concerned with trying to decide which table would be the best option to sit at to keep the waitress and any other customers from hearing their conversation.

"Let's take the back booth," he said, placing a hand on the small of her back as he led her to the booth farthest away from the front counter and the door.

Letting Baylin sit first, he slid into the opposite side of the booth.

"How are you two doing today?"

Looking away from Baylin's set face for not sitting next to her, Jody raised his eyes to the waitress.

He felt as if a thunderbolt had come from the ceiling to strike his nuts and could only stare at the woman, not making any move to accept the menu from her. Treepoint was a small town, so the fact he didn't recognize her told him that she was new to town. If the woman was meant to be important to his family or him, his brothers would have seen it in the stars. Because they hadn't, his inexplicable reaction to her shook him.

Seeing where his attention was centered, Baylin reached out to take both menus, laying his down in front of him.

"We're good," Baylin answered for them through tight lips.

"What can I get you this morning?" the waitress asked, giving them a friendly smile.

"We'll take two coffees," Baylin ordered.

"Okay, I'll get that for you." She smiled at Baylin then gave him a sympathetic glance, as if he wasn't all there. Jody couldn't blame her; he was acting like a dumbstruck idiot. "Look over the menu, and I'll take your orders when I come back."

From the reaction he was having, Jody could have sworn

he had just met his soul mate, if not for the fact her star was nowhere within sight of Treepoint.

Glancing away from the waitress as she walked away, he was met with Baylin's furious glare.

"Could you be more obvious?" she hissed at him.

"What?" He frowned in pretend ignorance.

"Don't act like you don't know what I'm talking about, Jody. For a second, I thought you were going to come when she smiled at you."

Fuck, he hadn't been that obvious, had he? He reassured himself that the only reason Baylin had read his reaction so easily was because he had spent several hours during the night fucking her.

Deciding the best way to respond to her accusation was not to, he picked up the menu to study it.

The waitress coming back with the coffee had him placing the menu down, keeping his eyes on Baylin as the coffee cups were placed on the table.

"Are you ready to order?"

"I'll take a BLT," Baylin ordered. "What about you, Jody?"

"I'll take the steak and eggs."

"How would you like your eggs?"

"Over medium."

"How do you like your steak cooked?"

"Medium," he managed to croak out. Why in the hell hadn't he ordered the same as Baylin?

"All right, I'll give the cook your order. Just let me know if you need more coffee."

Jody's eyes never left Baylin's, feeling a cold sweat run down his back. What the fuck was going on with him? The whole time the waitress had stood next to the table, he felt as if she were giving off a static charge. If he didn't know his soul mate wasn't supposed to appear in his life for another year, he could swear she was the one destined for him.

Picking up his cup of coffee, he put the waitress out of his mind. He had to deal with Baylin, sure his reaction to the waitress was only an intense physical attraction. Silas had warned him last year when he had stopped by unexpectedly to borrow his truck and found him with Mina that he was treading on thin ice where women were concerned. He had listened and stopped going into town to find the sexual release the women offered.

"I'm sorry I'm cramping your style."

His jaw clenched at the snide way Baylin was glaring at him.

"I wouldn't let you cramp my style if I were interested."

He had meant to wait until after they ate to talk to Baylin, but the way she was talking to him had him responding in kind. He didn't like being unkind, but when push came to shove, he was no pushover.

"You brought me here to break up with me, didn't you?"

At Baylin's raised voice, Jody looked toward the counter, seeing the waitress waiting on a lone customer. "Lower your voice."

"Don't want your waitress to hear?" Baylin's voice grew louder.

Jody leaned over the table, keeping his voice low. "If you think you can embarrass me, you won't. The only one who will be embarrassed is you. I'm a Coleman—I'm used to being trash-talked. Are you?"

Baylin's jaw snapped shut.

He used the opportunity to say what needed to be said.

"To break up, it would mean we are a couple—we aren't. I made that plain from the get-go. I wasn't looking for a commitment. What we did have was an arrangement that neither of us would get serious, both times we talked about it. You agreed each time. You're the one who is trying to take it from the bedroom to a relationship I clearly said was never going to happen," he told her coldly.

"Here you go."

Wanting to bite his tongue off when he looked up and saw the waitress standing there with their food, Jody had no choice but to brazen it out. "Thank you, Rowyn."

Frowning, he looked away to stare down at the food she had placed in front of him. Why did her name sound wrong on his lips? He had noticed her name sewn onto her uniform top when she had first come to their table. That was why he had been reassured she wasn't his soul mate.

"Is something wrong with your food?"

Jody raised his eyes back to hers.

Her friendly smile was gone as she stared back at him.

"No, it looks good. Thank you," he lied, looking away from the rare steak and runny eggs.

The waitress gave him a disparaging look before shifting her gaze to Baylin. "Is your food okay?" she asked sympathetically. "I can get you something else if you want."

"No, it's fine."

His lips tightened at Baylin's tearful expression. He should be the one crying. At least her burnt bacon didn't look like it was about to jump off her plate and start running.

"Can I freshen your coffee?"

"No, we're good," Jody answered for both of them.

The waitress gave Baylin time to gather herself, which Jody would have thought was sweet, if he wasn't coming across as the bad guy by breaking her heart.

The waitress ignored him, waiting for Baylin's answer.

"I'm fine. Would you mind bringing me a to-go box? I've lost my appetite."

"I'll be right back."

After giving him a warning look, the waitress briefly left them alone.

As soon as the waitress' back was turned, Baylin gave him a feline smile. "Good luck getting into her panties now."

Picking up his fork and knife, he started eating, afraid if he didn't keep his mouth full, he would say something he would regret.

From the way the waitress stared at him when she returned to the table with the to-go box, Baylin had accomplished her goal.

"I'll take the ticket."

Lowering his fork carefully to his plate, Jody caught Baylin's gaze. "I would stop while you're ahead," he warned, which had both women looking at him warily. "You can give me the ticket when I'm ready to leave." Remembering his manners, despite how angry he was, he gave the waitress a dismissive nod.

"We're good. If we need anything else, I'll let you know," Baylin said pitifully.

The waitress didn't immediately leave. "Are you okay?"

Baylin raised her napkin to her eyes, as if she were about to burst into tears. "I guess I'll have to be. Thank you."

Nodding, the waitress stepped away to wait on the customers who had just come in. Jody was conscious of her standing where she could keep an eye on their table while Baylin placed her food in the to-go container.

"So, this is it? I'm not going to see you anymore?"

Jody cut off a rare piece of his steak. Piercing it with his fork, he lifted his eyes to hers. "No chance in hell." Callously, Jody let her see exactly what her chances were of him ever knocking on her door again. "I don't know what you were going for by acting the way you did. Either you're a fucking psycho living in a dreamworld, or you did it to get back at me and used the waitress to even your scoreboard. Whatever the reason was, you miscalculated. Colemans might have a bad reputation in town, but no one says we're stupid, do they?"

Paling, Baylin grabbed her container and fled.

Determined to ride out the embarrassing situation, he ate his food until his churning stomach couldn't handle another bite. The only reason he had eaten the godawful food was because he wanted the least interaction with Rowyn as possible. Complaining about the food would have him talking more to her and having to wait for the food to be prepared all over again. Having to eat the revolting food was a price he was willing to pay to get away from Rowyn and the effect she had on him.

Standing, he went to the cash register. When she noticed him, the waitress finished pouring the coffee into a customer's cup.

"Was everything all right with your meal?" she asked him stiltedly, giving him the check.

"Yes." Lying, he took out his wallet. Pulling out the necessary cash, he handed the bills to her. "Keep the change."

"Thank you. Come again."

After the words left her mouth, her face turned bright red before she practically ran through the door to the kitchen to disappear.

He didn't have to wonder what had embarrassed the woman. It had been plain she had heard Baylin's remark.

Gritting his teeth, he jerked the door open. He couldn't have made a worse first impression if he'd tried. Thank goodness the waitress wasn't meant for him. Baylin had made him look like a dirtbag.

Well, Jody thought fatalistically, at least he had a year for the gossip to die down. The diner had been the hotbed of gossip before the last owner had taken it over. At least the current owner seemed more hospitable than Marty had been. Whoever they were, at least they allowed the customers to eat inside.

Pulling out onto the main road in Treepoint, he braked at

the red stop light. Jody drummed his fingers on the steering wheel. He saw only one slight problem—his reaction to Rowyn. Looking back, he was sure his reaction hadn't been as intense as he remembered it.

Shifting on the bench seat, he put the truck in gear when the light turned green. Who was he kidding? He was lusting after a woman when he shouldn't have after the night he had spent with Baylin. That in itself was a warning he needed to stay away from the waitress. The only one he wanted that reaction from was his soul mate.

Was that what Silas had been attempting to warn him about? If so, Silas should have given him a stronger warning other than to be careful that he was treading on thin ice.

It might be too late, but he was going to give the town a wide berth until his soul mate came to town.

As he drove up the mountain road toward his family's land, the sun was beginning to come up. When he passed The Last Riders' clubhouse, he saw there were already lights on and the members crossing the parking lot to head to the factory.

Three miles ahead, he put on his blinker, even though no one was on the road. The curvy road could be dangerous if someone wasn't paying attention to their speed. Making the turn into his family's driveway, he looked to the side of the yard and saw Silas and Fynn watching the sky where the last of the stars were making way for the sun's arrival.

A cold chill ran down his spine. His younger brother was in his pajamas instead of being inside, getting ready for school.

Jody could think of only one reason that Silas wouldn't have Fynn inside, getting ready, and that was if they needed to read the stars. Something had happened.

And with a clench of dread, Jody was afraid to find out what it was.

Chapter Four

"You need something?"

Sophie looked at the new cook she had hired blankly. She had never been so mortified in her whole life, and she'd experienced some standout embarrassing moments.

"No, I was going ..." Since she was standing next to the refrigerator, she opened the door. "I wanted to get more creamer," she invented the excuse quickly.

"I told you business would pick up once everyone saw the diner was open again," George wheezed out.

"Yes, you did."

Three customers weren't going to keep the lights on, but hopefully, as more people in town heard the diner was reopened, business would improve.

She took the box of creamers from the refrigerator and went back through the swinging door. After placing the creamers in the small refrigerator under the coffee station, she picked up the coffee pot to refill her customers' cups.

"Ready to order?"

The elderly man ordered a breakfast sampler.

Sophie inwardly groaned. She really needed to redo the menus she had found from the previous restaurant. The different foods offered on the breakfast sampler were just more chances for the cook to fail. She had meant to create a new menu last night, but she had been so tired by the time she made it back to her apartment that she decided washing her clothes was more of a priority.

At least the second day of opening the restaurant was going smoother than yesterday.

The opening had been a disaster from beginning to end. George, who she had hired after placing an ad in the town's newspaper for a cook, was just getting used to going back to work, she told herself. It wasn't like she had much choice in hiring him, since George had been the only person who applied. When he told her that he used to work at the diner before Marty bought it, she had hired him immediately. That was her first mistake. She should have tested his cooking skills.

The mistake had become apparent when she'd started getting complaints about the food from the few customers she served yesterday. Undercooked bacon, burnt biscuits, and what George had done to the meatloaf to make it taste so bad was a mystery she never wanted to solve.

To make matters worse, she was operating on a string-shoe budget until her mother and stepfather could move to Treepoint to help out.

At least, this morning she hadn't had any complaints about the food. She now wished she had hired a waitress instead of a cook—she couldn't do any worse at cooking than George. Once her parents arrived, her mother would take over the kitchen and her stepfather could help with the front of the restaurant. *If* she could survive financially until they got here in three weeks, and right now, the possibility of the restaurant supporting all three of them looked bleak.

She loved being a waitress. She had basically been raised in a variety of different restaurants. Her mom had told her that when she and Marty were married, she had placed a playpen in the kitchen of their restaurant. After her divorce, she taught her to sit out of way, at a table to play. She had grown up pretending to wait on customers until she was old enough to perform simple tasks to help out. How many years had she dreamed of owning her own restaurant, with her family working alongside her?

She wasn't going to give up that dream without a fight.

There was a downside to waitressing—she learned more about customers' lives than she wanted to know. Yesterday, she had overheard one of them telling her friend that she was going to leave her husband. It didn't seem right she was privy to that information before her husband. Today, listening to a woman being dumped and witnessing her reaction had been hard. Sadly, she had been in her place a time or two.

Sophie could understand why the woman appeared so devasted. The man who was dumping her was so hot she was shocked his ass hadn't set his chair on fire. It was everything she could do to close her mouth before approaching their table. Men who looked like him should be considered a fire hazard.

He was built like a linebacker, the material of his T-shirt straining to cover his biceps and chest. His girlfriend was no slouch, either, dressed as if she were about to go the gym. The black workout top she wore under her jacket had shown a sleekly toned midriff and pert breasts surpassing of her bra. Sophie had stared at the woman's generous display in envy. And not for the first time did she consider getting breast implants.

Her girls weren't totally lacking, but they weren't va-va vroom, either. Just once she wanted to be va-va vroom. Her friend, Talia, was without trying. Sophie had complained to her on more than one occasion, mainly when they were drunk off their asses. She had to work to be a va; she inspired to be a va-va. To be a va-va vroom, she would have to go to one of those expensive plastic surgeons in California. Talia was a natural va-va vroom, and if she weren't so nice, Sophie would hate her.

Her envy of her female customer had vanished before she could get three steps away from the couple. The woman had accused him of staring at her as if just looking at her would make him come. Her legs had nearly buckled under her when she'd heard that shattering tidbit because. If his girlfriend had been aware that her body had reacted the same way, the only tip she would have gotten was to run.

Sophie had noticed the woman's stiletto-shaped bloodred nails. She didn't want those things anywhere near her face. Having to psych herself to go back to take their order hadn't been easy, and she couldn't have done so at a worse moment.

Whatever the relationship the woman had thought she was having with the man wasn't the same as he wanted. From her expression, the woman had been crushed.

Sophie would bet a hundred bucks the guy waited until he had scored before hitting the end button.

Why did men have to be such rat bastards? The guy seemed comfortable smashing the woman's heart, too comfortable from her point of view. In her opinion, way too indifferent.

Her mind played back the woman's heartbreak, and she unintentionally glared down at the customer whose order she was taking.

Other than the woman's nails, she had seemed nice. Sophie could even see them become friends in the future. They could compare skid marks where their lousy exes had run over them.

Returning her glare, the customer lowered his menu back to the table. "You the new owner?"

"Yes." Belatedly, she realized she had made the customer the recipient of her frustration for the male species.

"I heard you're Marty's daughter."

"Yes."

The customer looked at his friend. "That apple didn't fall from the tree, did it?"

Sophie hadn't seen her father for the last years of his life but knew she didn't resemble Marty. She didn't have to take a wild guess that her customer wasn't talking about the physical similarities she shared with her father.

Within five minutes of her arriving in town, she had discovered the town's hatred for him. She couldn't blame them; Marty's only redeemable part was his ability to fry a damn good burger.

"I apologize for my rudeness. I had something else on my mind. I didn't mean to take it out on you," she apologized.

Both men stared at her in shock.

"Marty would have let the restaurant burn down before he apologized." The man held out his hand. "Moon." He then gestured to the man across the table. "This is Train."

"Sophie. It's nice to meet you both," she introduced herself with a lopsided grin. "I heard my father didn't have the best customer service skills."

"Nonexistent would be closer to the mark."

She took their order and retreated from their table.

Placing the ticket in kitchen window, she peeked through the opening to see what George was doing.

"George!" she said loudly. "Wake up."

The old man jerked. "Fuck. You trying to scare me to death?"

"No. I was trying to keep you from taking a nosedive onto the grill," she told him sharply.

"I wasn't sleeping," he denied.

Sophie wasn't going to argue over the fact he was. Next time, she would just let him fry himself.

"I put up an order."

Turning away from the window, she promised herself that, before the end of the day, she was going to run another ad. Customers already didn't want to eat here because of Sophie's father's reputation of being a foul-mouthed, hateful son-of-bitch. The last she needed was to have to deal with the cook's inept skills. The way she was going, she'd put the restaurant out of business during the same week it opened.

Thinking about the restaurant going bust had her worried. Every dime of her savings had gone into stocking the restaurant, turning the utilities back on, and renting an apartment. She didn't have a safety margin.

Her parents had already given their notice and were packing to move to Treepoint. If she failed, they would be left high and dry.

Cut it out, Sophie, she scolded herself. *You're going to make it.* She needed confidence right now, not doom and gloom.

"Order up!" George yelled out.

Sophie returned to the window to stare at the food George had put there.

God help her, everything was going to hell in a handbasket.

Chapter Five

Parking his truck in the driveway, Jody walked to where Silas and Fynn were standing.

"What's going on?" he asked his eldest brother. "Why isn't Fynn getting ready for school?"

Silas' craggy face turned toward him. At his expression, Jody knew he was in trouble, though he didn't know what he'd done when he hadn't even been home.

"What'd I do?"

"Fynn, go get ready for school."

Fynn gave him a sympathetic glance as he headed for the main house.

"I wasn't supposed to be here for another thirty minutes—"

"Where were you last night?" Silas' solemn voice cut him off.

"I'm not a kid anymore, Silas. Where I spent the night isn't any of your business."

Silas' inscrutable expression became even more withdrawn. "Fine." His brother started toward the house.

"Wait." Jody started after him. "Why did you have Fynn out, reading the sky?"

"I was double-checking something."

"What were you double-checking?"

"Nothing pertaining to me, or the others."

"You saw something that would affect *me*? What was it?"

Silas went up the steps to the house. "Like you said, you're not a kid anymore. Find out for yourself."

Shit, he had pissed Silas off.

Instead of following him inside, Jody strode off in the direction of his trailer. When Silas was angry, it wouldn't do any good to badger him. He was a great believer in the live-and-learn philosophy.

Dammit. Jody kicked a large stick out of his way. He knew better than to give Silas attitude. Being the oldest of ten kids of a single father, Silas had borne the responsibility of caring for the younger children. After their father and little sister had died in an accident, he took on the full-time responsibility of their family without complaint. Jody didn't think he would have had the capacity to handle the obligations of putting a roof over their heads and food on the table for so many children, all the while experiencing his own grief, as Silas had done.

Silas had always been the more serious of his siblings. After the accident, he had grown even more somber.

Reaching his trailer, Jody changed from his jeans and T-shirt to gray cargo pants and an orange hoodie. After putting on a thick pair of socks, he laced up his boots before heading out of the door. With five minutes to spare, he rushed to where he was meeting up with his brothers for the job they had been hired to do for the day.

His brothers were gathered around Matthew and Isaac's workshop. When he felt the focus of their gazes, his eyes automatically went to Jacob—they had a close bond and looked out for each other. Reading the caution in his eyes, Jody walked to where he was standing to listen to what Silas was saying.

"We need to have the fence installed by lunchtime."

Was Silas talking about the job in the new housing subdivision? How in the fuck were they supposed to get it done in four hours? Not about to ask Silas the question and draw his ire again, Jody remained silent.

Thankfully, Jacob didn't feel the same restraint.

"That's a three-day job; what's the hurry?"

"This morning, we're going to be working on the job. Then Matthew, Isaac, Jacob, and Reaper will be finishing the other job."

What other job didn't he know about?

"What will the rest of you be doing?" Jacob frowned. "Matthew said his next order won't be ready until next week."

Instead of looking at Jacob, Silas stared at Jody. "We'll be working at the diner."

Jody's mouth dropped open.

Unable to wait for Jacob or one of his other brothers to ask the question burning in his mind, he asked it himself. "What will we be doing at the diner?"

"Whatever the new owner needs us to do. She is having trouble settling in and needs our help before she becomes discouraged and sells the diner."

From Jody's perspective, he wanted the woman to sell and leave town. The sooner, the better. Especially before his soul mate came to town.

"What does it matter if she does?"

Silas arched an eyebrow in his direction. "It doesn't matter to me if she does, but you might care. The owner is your soul mate."

Jody started shaking his head. "She isn't my soul mate."

As the words came out of his mouth, he felt the truth in his bones.

Turning around so his brothers couldn't see his face, Jody recalled the reaction he'd had when he saw her for the first time. His soul and body had recognized her as his mate; it'd been his damn ego that had let him down. Silas had warned him numerous times that his hookups were going to bite him in his ass.

"She is," Silas argued firmly from behind his back.

Jody turned back around. "I met her this morning."

All of his brothers stared at him with curious eyes, except for Silas.

"When did you find out?" he asked him.

"This morning when I woke up. I saw the stars becoming clearer. I woke Fynn up. He was telling me what he saw when you came home."

"The stars didn't want me to know ahead of time."

"No, they didn't," Silas agreed. "It was the first time since before Greer's stroke that I could see her here."

Jody stared at Silas sympathetically. Silas had read the stars after Matthew's soul mate had arrived in town. Silas' soul mate's star was also moving closer to his, which meant Silas and his soul mate would soon be together.

After Greer's stroke, Silas' soul mate's star had moved further away. Silas had said it was his punishment for using his gift to warn Matthew's wife that she was in danger and prevented her from being killed by a man who had tormented her since childhood.

"I didn't make the best first impression," Jody admitted to his brothers.

Jacob looked as if he wasn't surprised. "What happened?"

"I took Baylin to the diner to have breakfast and had to end up telling her I wasn't going to see her anymore. I didn't break it to her gently. Baylin was making out like we were a couple. I got angry," he explained curtly. "The waitress had a first-row seat."

Jacob and Isaac grimaced, Matthew broke into laughter, while Silas remained stoic.

"I told you Treepoint was too small of a town to cat around in," Matthew rubbed it in like salt in a wound.

Jody glared at Matthew. "The last thing I want to hear right now is *I told you so*."

Matthew arched his brows at him. "You didn't have a problem making fun of me for staying home when you and Isaac went out."

Jody knew it would be a total waste of time to continue arguing with Matthew. Instead, he looked at Silas for guidance. "How can I fix it?"

"You're on your own where that's concerned. My main concern is that she stays in town. If she closes the diner down and leaves town, that's going to put us out of order for our soul mates." His expression turned disconsolate.

Jamming his hands into his pockets, Jody felt terrible about how Silas' soul mate had moved farther away from him. His brother had sacrificed his own happiness more than once to benefit their family. He deserved his own family rather than making sure they were taken care of. They were all grown men except for Fynn; it was time they stopped relying so heavily on Silas.

"I'm sorry, bro." Jody placed a hand on Silas' shoulder. "I fucked up. You warned me, and I didn't listen. This morning, I acted like an ass to you because, deep down, I knew who she was, and I didn't want to admit it because it was easier to not acknowledge what I was feeling rather than admitting I had screwed up. I'll fix it. I swear."

Changing his solemn tone to one more cheerful, he gazed toward his brothers, whose expressions had turned serious when Silas had said Jody's soul mate leaving would affect their own soul mates.

"I might have fucked up, but that doesn't mean I'm down for the count. I'm not afraid of a challenge." At this point, he didn't know if he was trying to ease his brothers' worries or his own, but he went all-in. "Once I turn my charm on her, she'll fall in love with me like that." Jody snapped his fingers confidently.

All of his brothers stared at him doubtfully.

"We're so fucked," Isaac muttered under his breath.

Jody didn't appreciate Isaac's lack of confidence, especially since his older brother wasn't so innocent himself.

"You all go on to the housing development. I've got this," he assured them, giving Isaac a glare, which dared him to say anything else. "I'll let you know when the wedding is," he told them overconfidently.

His brothers shrugged despite their dubious expressions. Disbanding, they went into Matthew and Isaac's workshop before coming back out to load their trucks with the iron fencing.

"If you change your mind, call, and we'll come over," Silas told him, remaining by his side.

"You worry too much." Jody gave Silas a brotherly smack on his back before turning to go back to his trailer.

"Where are you going? I thought you were going to the diner?"

"I have to change first. I'm not going to nab the girl wearing this get-up. I have to make a better impression."

Jody couldn't make out what Silas muttered under his breath. "What did you say?"

"I said, I'm going to die a bachelor."

Chapter Six

J ody was about to open the door to the diner when it was opened from the inside. Moving aside to let Moon and Train pass, he noticed neither of The Last Riders looked happy.

"Moon, Train," he greeted the Last Riders.

"If you're going in to eat, save your money. We sent our food back three times, and she still couldn't get it right," Moon complained.

"They're probably just having a bad day."

"I heard yesterday wasn't much better," Train derided. "All I wanted was pancakes. I ended up eating burnt toast."

Jody's stomach churned, remembering his own breakfast.

"They're probably just overwhelmed with opening a new business. I'm sure it'll get better."

Train didn't mince words. "If two customers overwhelm them, I don't see it getting much better."

Unable to come up with another explanation for the bad food, he let The Last Riders go on their way.

Before he could make another attempt to open the door, it opened again. An old man came out with an angry expression.

"We'll see how good she does without me," Jody heard the old man complain as he walked past him.

Damn. Silas wasn't going to be the only one to die a bachelor with the way the diner was sinking fast.

He waited until he was sure no one else was coming out of the diner before he opened the door. The restaurant was empty. He couldn't see the waitress, either.

Walking to the front counter, he took a seat. He had hoped the waitress would have seen him entering. He looked good, he thought to himself.

He was dressed in his nicest jeans and boots and wore a blue shirt that his sister, Ginny, had told him highlighted the blue in his eyes; Jody felt confident he would be able to sweep his soul mate off her feet ... once he charmed her into forgetting the little breakup he'd had with Baylin a couple of hours before.

Jody was growing worried when he sat there for several minutes without seeing her.

When she finally came out of the back, however, she appeared startled to find him there.

"I'm sorry. I didn't hear you come in," she apologized, red flooding her cheeks.

"No problem. I'm in no hurry." He gave her a smile he had practiced in his bathroom mirror while he shaved.

Her eyes narrowed on him suspiciously. Jody didn't take that as a good sign.

Damn. The woman was going to be a hard nut to crack.

"Can I get you something?"

"I'll take a cup of coffee," he ordered.

She went to the coffee machine.

Telling himself not to become discouraged, he kept his smile on his lips.

When she returned with his coffee, he took the opportunity to introduce himself. "I'm Jody Coleman. What's your name?"

Frost covered her features as she pointed at the name on her uniform.

"You don't look like a Rowyn to me," he teased.

When she set the coffee cup down in front of him, Jody could see the muscles in her jaw tense.

"What's a Rowyn supposed to look like?"

"I don't know. Someone uppity?" Feeling as if the ground was sinking beneath him, he tried to regain his footing. "I'm just a country boy." Jody inwardly winced at the words coming out of his mouth. "What do your friends call you?"

"Since you're not my friend, it's none of your business," she told him coldly.

"Ouch." He placed a hand over his heart. "You're right; it's none of my business. I was just making friendly conversation."

"I'm sorry. I'm not having a great day. I didn't mean to take it out on you. I just had to fire my cook. I'm not great at taking a job away from someone who needs it."

"Don't feel bad about firing him. A cook has to know how to make toast."

The waitress' face went back to red. "The toast was my fault. George told me the toaster was getting stuck. I didn't want to spend the money to buy a new one."

"Oh ... um ..." Jody tried to think of something else to say.

"It's okay." She must have seen the dilemma on his face. "I know the toast was my fault. The pancakes, which got him fired, were his. Can I get you something else?"

"No, I'm good."

Nodding, she went to sit down at one of the booths to do something on her cell phone.

As he drank his coffee, Jody tried to think of something to say that would start a conversation between them.

"How do you like living in Treepoint so far?"

"Fine."

How had he ever gotten laid with his conversation skills?

Taking another sip of his coffee, he hoped someone would come in to get her out of the booth. It was hard talking to someone who was ignoring him.

"I'm sorry for the loss of your father."

"Don't be."

His shoulders sank. Obviously, her father was no great loss to her.

"Treepoint will grow on you." Deciding to talk to her as if she did want to talk to him, he barreled ahead. "There're a lot of fun things to do here."

"Like what?"

Why in the hell had he just shot himself in the foot? There wasn't jackshit to do in Treepoint. The point was to make her want to stay, not to convince her to leave.

"There's a nice movie theater and really nice steak restaurant across the str ..." His voice dropped off as he realized what he was saying. Using another restaurant as an enticement to stay might not have been the best route to take. From the way she looked at him, as if he was slow on the uptake, he couldn't blame her. Why was he having such a hard time talking to her? He'd never had this problem before.

The stars might say they are soul mates, but she wasn't the woman he had imagined since he had found out about her existence.

She was a brunette instead of a blonde, nor was she particularly pretty. If not for the effect she had on his body whenever she came near him, he would have passed her off as uninteresting. There was nothing eye-catching about her. She hadn't made the effort to put on any makeup, and her hair was pulled back into a tight bun.

Unless he was wrong, which wasn't likely, her breasts were

a thirty-two double A. He had noticed she had a nice smile when she had smiled at Baylin.

"Would you like a refill?"

"Thanks." Jody lifted the cup as she got up out of the booth, taking a long drink and nearly burning his tongue off.

Scooting the cup forward, he gave her another one of his practiced smiles. "I would be happy to drive you around town when you get off and show you everything."

As she poured the coffee, she lifted her eyes from the cup. "I've already become familiar with Treepoint. There wasn't much to see. There are two apartment complexes here, one of which I rent from; a school; a courthouse; three dine-in restaurants, including this one; two convenience stores; two department stores, a shoe store, and four office buildings."

"You missed the hotel," he joked. "You have trouble finding a place to live? Housing is in short supply here. I could help you find a place—"

"No, thanks. Like I said, I already found an apartment, at the Omni."

Jody felt a lump form in his throat. Baylin lived at the Omni.

"It's close to here. I'm on the third floor."

Baylin's apartment was on the third floor.

Jody thought back to last night. Had she seen them as they entered the building?

"It even has its own laundry facilities, right in the middle of the third floor, to make it convenient for everyone. All I have to do is open my door and walk across the hall to wash my clothes."

The lump settled firmly in his throat, making it impossible to talk. Across the hall from Baylin's apartment was the laundry facility. That meant his soul mate lived next to Baylin.

He was unable to meet her knowing gaze, so his eyes dropped to his coffee. He didn't have to ask if Baylin's bedroom wall connected to hers. The way his luck was running, it did.

Jody felt his cheeks redden as he remembered the loud noises they had made the previous evening.

"The best part is everyone seems to wash their clothes during the day. Last evening, I had the laundry room to myself."

The laundry room didn't have a door for the safety of the tenants. He had been seen and heard last night.

Jody knew it would be a waste of time to continue, so he took his wallet out of his pocket. Placing a ten on the counter, he stood up. "Keep the change."

"Thanks."

Jody could have sworn he heard the undertone of laughter in her voice as he left the diner.

He went to his truck and pulled out his cell phone. It was time to call in the cavalry.

Chapter Seven

Sophie stared around the empty restaurant. Then, after taking a notebook she kept under the counter, she sat down. Opening the notebook, she scanned through the figures she had tallied for her expenditures. She flipped the pages until she came to the end tally. She had a whopping fifty dollars left.

Crying, she buried her face in her hands just as the bell rang over the door, indicating a customer's arrival.

When she lifted her face, her jaw dropped at seeing a group of men walking inside. Stunned at the sight, she sat motionless as they filed in, filling the large round table in the middle of the restaurant. Closing the notebook, she turned her face from gawking at the men to wipe the tears from her face.

She recognized one of the faces as she approached the table but focused on the one who seemed to be the oldest, who was staring at her with a comforting gaze.

"I'm sorry, gentlemen, I have to close for the day. I don't have a cook."

"We're working at the housing development not far from here. We're putting up a fence around the development. Ma'am, we're thirsty and hungry. My brothers are used to eating anything you put in front of us. They could make the drinks for us, if you could find it in your heart to find something to eat."

"I can do that."

Sophie found herself in the kitchen, staring wonderingly at what she was doing. Before the men had shown up, she was about to call one of the realtors in town.

Sighing, she opened the door of the refrigerator. She had plenty of hamburger meat. She pulled some out, turned on the grill, and started putting the patties on. Then she turned on the fryer and went to the freezer to take out a bag of fries. Waiting until the burgers were done on one side, she flipped them then dropped a basket of fries into the hot oil.

She wasn't a great cook, but she knew how to prepare the staples. If she thought George could be able to waitress, she would have taken over the kitchen and let him serve, but her skills were mediocre at best. She needed an exceptional cook if she was going to make this restaurant work.

Her mother was an exceptional cook. She just needed time for her parents to get here.

Opening the pack of buns, she placed them down on the grill to warm them. Marty might have been a terrible father, but he had taught her how to make hamburgers and fries.

Pulling the fries out of the oil, she seasoned them under the warming lights, then took the buns off the grill and started to assemble the hamburgers before placing them on plates. Once she was done, she added a hefty portion of fries to each plate.

She was about to carry two plates out to the men after placing three in the window when she saw Jody remove the three plates.

"I thought you could use some help," he said with a grin.

With the window empty, she placed the two she was holding there before picking up the last three. As she carried them through the kitchen door, she saw another man taking the ones from the window.

Jody met her halfway, taking the two plates she was holding on one arm.

"Thank you."

"You're welcome."

He set one of the plates down in front of the man who was sitting next to his empty chair. Then Jody sat down at the table.

"Can I get any of you some more drinks?"

The older man, who had convinced her to make them something to eat, motioned to one of the men. "Jacob topped all our drinks off already. Please, sit with us as we eat."

One of the other men motioned to a wedged-in empty chair next to the man who seemed to be the spokesman for the family.

Since there was no one else in the restaurant, she sat down with the group of men, telling herself that she needed to be friendly with her customers if she was going to make a living out of the restaurant, conveniently forgetting she had decided to sell the restaurant before the men had arrived.

"You must think we're heathens for not introducing ourselves." The oldest one smiled at her. "I'm Silas Coleman, and these are my brothers, Matthew, Isaac, Jody—whom I believe you've already met—Jacob, Moses, and Ezra."

Sophie stared around the table as Silas pointed at each brother as he introduced them.

"It's nice to meet you all. I'm Sophie."

Jody stared pointedly at her nametag. "I knew the name on your uniform didn't fit."

"I found the top out back. I ordered a nametag; it hasn't come yet."

"It's a pleasure to meet you," Silas responded then frowned down at the food in front of him.

"Is something wrong with the food?" She bit her lip, noticing he hadn't touched his.

Silas' frown cleared. "Not at all, ma'am. It's just ... I seem to have lost my appetite. Here." He slid his plate in front of her. "You mind joining us for lunch? I'll just grab a cup of coffee, if you don't mind."

"I can—" Sophie started to get up, but Silas placed a hand on her shoulder. "I can get it myself. Eat the burger before it gets cold."

Hearing the command in his voice, she picked up the hamburger as Silas got up from the table. The men didn't start eating until she picked up hers.

Across the table, her eyes met Jody's. She blushed and lowered her eyes to the burger as she took a bite.

All she had eaten yesterday was ramen noodles, sick to her stomach at how the day had gone. Today, she had meant to eat some toast but didn't have the stomach for it, knowing she was going to have to fire George.

Silas resumed his seat, holding a cup of coffee. "Everyone in town has been anxious for the diner to reopen," he told her. "King makes a good steak, but his hamburgers are too thick, and he doesn't open for breakfast."

Sophie swallowed her bite of food. "I won't be able to, either, until I can find a cook. No one else has applied. I can cook a few things, like hamburgers and fries. But most of the things people want to eat here are country cooking. I've worked in restaurants before, but they've been mainly fast food places. I was so anxious to open the restaurant that I didn't think it through," she revealed without knowing why she was confiding to a group of strangers. Their sympathetic gazes had her continuing.

"My mother can cook anything. Her mom had a restaurant, and she used to own one when she was married to Marty. When she comes to town, she and my stepfather will be able to help me manage the restaurant."

"That sounds like a fine plan." Silas nodded, taking a sip of his coffee.

"Except I'll be bankrupt before they get here. I was thinking of calling a realtor."

"You shouldn't make any hasty decisions," Jody blurted out from across the table.

Sophie saw Silas giving Jody a quelling look.

"The boys seem to be enjoying the hamburgers and fries. Maybe if you just focus on the items on the menu you're comfortable making, you won't need to hire a cook."

"I can try that," she agreed. "It's not like I'm being overrun with customers, anyway."

"The customers will come back once you provide them with friendly service and good food."

She took another bite as she listened to Silas, trying to keep her eyes fixed on him instead of the male candy seated around the table.

It wasn't as if Silas wasn't as handsome as his brothers, but he put out a brotherly vibe. The other men at the table oozed testosterone. The one seated next to Jody kept drawing her eyes. Sophie remembered his name was Isaac.

Hastily looking down at her plate when she caught Jody glowering at her for staring at Isaac, she dipped her fries into the ketchup and turned her mind back to what Silas was saying.

"We'd be happy to help out any way we can. My sister used to work at the diner before she got married. I'll have her stop by and give you some pointers about drawing the customers back. Jody and Jacob are at a loose end once we get this current job done. If you get busy and need some help, they can swing by and pitch in."

Sophie leaned back in her chair. "Thank you, but I can't accept your help. I'll be lucky to keep the lights on until my parents get here."

"My brothers don't expect any money."

Sophie stared at Silas suspiciously. Why would a stranger help her out? The lawyer had warned her about some of Marty's accomplices attempting to befriend her.

"Kentuckians might be known for their bourbon, but we couldn't hold our heads up if we didn't show you some southern hospitality," Silas told her, his reassuring voice soothing her fear that she wouldn't be able to keep the restaurant afloat. "Don't worry; just think of us as your new Kentucky family."

"Thank you, but I couldn't impose on your kindness." Sophie couldn't resist a lingering look toward Isaac. The last thing she thought about when she stared at the gorgeous males sitting around the table was family. "I appreciate the hospitality you've shown me."

Silas nodded. "Just keep my offer in mind. If you need anything, just reach out to me. One of the boys or I can be here in a few minutes. When I check out, I'll leave our numbers and Ginny's. She'd be a big help until your parents get here."

"I'll keep that in mind," she said with a smile.

Silas looked toward his brothers. "If you're done, we better get back to work."

When the men stood up, Sophie did, too, to go behind the counter to the cash register.

Silas approached the register as the men stood behind him. Taking out his wallet, he waited for her to give him the total.

Sophie did, which was half as much as she should have charged for the food.

"Ma'am, you need to check your register. That doesn't seem like you charged me enough."

Sophie smiled at him. "I gave you the family discount."

Chapter Eight

"You're so fucked," Isaac joked as they reached the parking lot.

"I am not."

"Seemed that way to me, too," Matthew agreed, taking Isaac's side. "There was only one man at the table she had eyes for, and it was not you."

Jody glared at his brothers. "She noticed me."

Jacob gave him a pitying glance. "Yeah, when you asked for the ketchup."

"You too, Jacob?"

"Sorry, bro, but it was hard to miss."

Jody wanted to grind his teeth but was too conscious about how much money Silas had spent fixing them. "She'll warm up to me."

Moses gave him a consoling pat on his shoulder. "You know I'm in your corner, but unless there is a freak snowstorm where we get ten inches of snow, and her electric goes out, she isn't going to be warming up anytime soon."

"Don't worry, Jody." Isaac gave him a mock serious look. "I'll throw her back your way if she hits on me."

Jody narrowed his eyes on his other brother. "I'm confident in my game. How about you, Isaac? You might have the prettier face, but we both know who the ladies come to when they want a touchdown."

Silas gave Isaac and him dark looks. "I wouldn't be bragging about who scored the most touchdowns. I've warned both of you that just because you know you have soul mates, that doesn't mean you'll end up with them. Dad never got his."

All of his brothers turned serious.

Grief filled Jody's heart. There wasn't a day that went by that he didn't miss his father. Freddy was the type of father other children wished they had. He had his own way of looking at things, which was why he had homeschooled them, disciplined them with love, and never let them forget how much he loved them.

"We need to get back to work and get as much done as possible today," Silas said, taking out his truck keys. "Jody, you might as well come with us. You can try again tomorrow."

Morosely, Jody got in his truck while the others piled into Silas and Matthew's trucks. He couldn't blame his brothers. If Sophie believed he was a player, then they could be tarnished by the same brush. While he wasn't the only Coleman brother who hadn't waited for his soul mate to appear, Isaac and Ezra were much more circumspect than he had been. They went further afield to do their fooling around.

When they arrived at the housing development, they all continued setting the fence. Jody took over digging the holes while Matthew and Isaac placed them. Silas would mix the concrete, then Ezra and Moses would place the iron posts in place. The work was backbreaking, and they had only made it less than halfway when Silas called them to a stop.

On the drive home, he was tempted to stop at the diner

again as he drove past. Wrinkling his nose at his sweat-dampened shirt, Jody decided he was better off not going.

"You going to eat at the house tonight?" Silas asked as he got out of his truck.

Jody slammed his truck door shut. "No, thanks. I'm going to make a sandwich and get to bed early tonight."

The rest of his brothers made their way to their own homes, all of them walking next to him.

"You're not going to see Sophie again today?" Jacob asked, following in step with him.

"Nah. Coming on too strong is the worst thing I can do."

Jacob nodded. "That's true, but it also gives someone else the opportunity to make their move."

Jody shot Isaac a warning glance. "As long as Isaac stays here, I'm good."

"Brother"—Isaac shrugged—"I wouldn't think of stepping on your toes."

Jody believed him. While they might tease each other, none of his brothers would ever try to steal his woman.

They reached the part of the property where he had to veer away from his brothers, and he told them good night. Going through the woods, it took him five minutes to reach his trailer. Jacob's wasn't far from his, a corpse of trees separating them.

Sighing as he went up the steps, he went inside. He looked around the trailer through different eyes. He had been saving his money. Now that his soul mate was near, it was time to decide if he was going to buy a bigger trailer or build a house, like Matthew had done. He would talk it over with Silas and get his advice for which one would make Sophie happier.

Walking into his bedroom, he removed his sweaty clothes. When he had started digging the holes, he had removed his nice shirt, but his new boots were trashed. Reminding himself to buy a new pair, he went into the bathroom to take a hot shower, letting the warm water work the knots out of his shoulders.

Afterward, he dressed in comfortable sweatpants, a T-shirt, and tennis shoes. Then he left the trailer and made his way to his sister's property. When he knocked on her door, he heard a grumpy voice call out for him to come inside.

Jody opened the door, immediately wishing he had called first. If he had heard the racket taking place in Ginny's house, he would have stayed home.

Ginny's husband was rocking his screaming daughter in the crook of his arm while his son was screeching along to a song being played on the television. He immediately started back out of the door.

"Sorry, I'll come back another time."

"Don't even think about it." Reaper's gaze pinned him in place.

Before he could take another step backward, Jody felt Reaper thrust the baby into his arms.

"I need a break." With that, Reaper bent down to lift his son into his arms, giving his rosy cheek a kiss. "You mind Jody until I get back."

Rocking Leah against his chest, he watched as Reaper set Freddie back down on his feet before going for the door.

"When are you coming back?" Jody asked him helplessly.

"Call me when Ginny gets back."

After watching the door for several minutes, Jody realized Reaper wasn't joking when he heard his motorcycle roaring away.

Jody stared down at his nephew, who was staring up at him with innocent eyes. "How long have you made your dad listen to that song?"

Freddie's rosy cheeks turned redder. "It's my favorite song. Will you sing with me?"

"No ..." Jody shook his head, moving to the couch to sit

down. Bouncing the fussy baby on his knee, he looked down in dismay when Leah rewarded him by dribbling spit up on him. Grabbing a baby wipe, he cleaned her up before cleaning his pants.

When he heard the door open, he was relieved to see Ginny coming through the door. His sister started laughing at seeing him sitting there instead of Reaper.

Jody got up, switching the grocery bags with Ginny to give her the crying baby.

"How did Reaper talk you into coming over?" she asked, taking Leah into her arms.

"He didn't give me a choice. I stopped by to see you, and the next thing I knew, I was holding Leah and Reaper was gone."

Ginny laughed harder. "Leah has been teething. I did the same thing when he came in from helping you guys."

"I don't know what's worse: the crying or the song," Jody said over his shoulder as he carried the grocery bags to the kitchen. He put the cold items in the fridge but left the other groceries for Ginny to put away.

"The song." Ginny had already turned the television off by the time he came back to the living room. "Freddie, play with your fort for a little while," she directed her son.

Watching as her son plopped down next to his toy box, Jody admired how quickly she regained control of the chaos.

Ginny sat down on a chair to place Leah on her shoulder, patting her back lovingly while eyeing him. "Did you need something?"

Jody sat down on the couch in front of her. "I can't just stop by to say hi?"

Ginny raised a disbelieving brow.

Jody grimaced. "I need a favor."

"What do you need?"

"The diner has reopened."

"I heard."

"The owner is my soul mate."

"Silas told me."

"He also tell you I screwed up?"

"Yes. You want me to go by and convince her what a great guy you are?"

"It would be nice if you could slip in compliments about me, but I mainly wanted you to help her get on her feet."

Ginny gave him one of her sweet smiles. "I'd be happy to do for that for you."

Jody released a relieved sigh. "Thanks, Ginny. I knew I could count on you."

"Of course, I'm going to need a babysitter."

Chapter Nine

S ophie felt in a better frame of mind as the men walked out the door. How many times had she wished for a brother? Always envious of her friends when they complained about theirs, she had seen the affection between the siblings despite their complaints.

Rounding the counter, she started cleaning the table. When she picked up Silas' coffee cup, she saw the bill placed underneath. Sure she was mistaken, she unfolded it to see it was a hundred-dollar bill.

She shook her head as she cleaned the rest of the table, finding a hundred-dollar bill under each plate. Placing the dishes in the plastic bin, she sniffed back tears as she stuffed the bills in her apron pocket.

She would have to return the money when they came in the next time. There was no way she could accept it, sure they had only given it to her because they had walked in while she'd been crying.

After wiping the table down, she went into the kitchen to load the dishwasher.

When she heard the bell over the door ring, she left the

kitchen, feeling more confident that she might be able to convince them to order hamburgers.

There was a lone man sitting in a corner booth. Pasting a smile on her face, she went over to greet him. As she drew closer, however, her smile slipped. He gave her the heebie-jeebies, making her want to run and hide behind the counter.

Looking through the window, she assured herself that the sheriff's office was just a few yards away.

"Hello, how are you doing today?"

The man's face was messed up to hell and back. His lips were huge, his cheeks were heavily pockmarked, and he had sagging flesh down his neck. He noticed her reaction, and his lips twisted in a sneer, making him appear even more sinister.

"Had better."

"What can I get you?"

"A large glass of iced tea, and I'll take the money your old man owes me."

Sophie locked her knees, afraid they would give out from under her. "I can get you the tea, but any money my father owes you, you'll have to talk to his lawyer. I can save you the trouble—once Marty's creditors were paid, there wasn't any money left."

"I'll take that tea."

She walked away on trembling legs and went behind the counter to fill the glass with ice and tea. Carrying it back, she had to concentrate on not to spill it as she gauged the distance to the door if she needed to run.

Setting the glass down, she forced herself to ask him if he wanted something else.

"Have a seat before you pass out."

She wished another customer would come in to give her an excuse to ignore him, but her hopes were dashed when the door remained closed.

Sitting down, she folded her hands over each other so he

wouldn't notice them shaking. "How much money does my father owe you?"

"Two hundred thousand."

Sophie felt the color drain out of her face. "I don't know what to tell you. Marty didn't leave me any money. The only thing I can say is to talk to his lawyer. I can get you his name and number."

"The money Marty owes me can't be discussed with a lawyer, nor can I take it to a court. I lent Marty the money in good faith. I want it back."

"If you're expecting me to give you the money, I don't have any. Look around—the place is empty. I can't even hire a cook. All the equipment is old, and the building isn't in better shape."

"It seems like we're at an impasse, then." Lifting the glass to his twisted lips, he drained its contents before placing it back down, then stood up. He was a scary figure. Taking out a wad of bills, he slammed a five down onto the table. "I would figure out how you're going to pay me before I come back. I'll be in touch."

Sophie watched him leave, shaking in terror. He scared the bejesus out of her.

Glancing toward the sheriff's office, she debated calling to make a report.

What could she say? He hadn't outright threatened her, just asked for his money. While he scared her, it was more the impression he gave her than anything overt he had done. Reaching for the empty glass, she carried it back to the kitchen.

She was beginning to dislike Treepoint. The only good thing that had happened to her since coming here was meeting Silas. His brother Isaac wasn't anything to sneeze at, either. It was a shame Jody was their brother. She wondered if the rest of his brothers were as heartless with women as he was.

This morning, when she had served him and the woman he was with, she hadn't realized it was the same couple she had seen the night before, smashing into the wall as they tried to get into the apartment across from the laundry room. She had put two and two together when she ducked out of the restaurant and ran home to allow the delivery drivers inside to bring in her couch and saw the woman going into the apartment.

Sighing, she started the dishwasher. It didn't matter regardless. The way her luck was running, she would be out of business long before she found out.

"Two hundred thousand dollars?" she said out loud. "Marty, what have you done?"

Chapter Ten

She was again debating with herself if she should close the restaurant to cross the street to the sheriff's office when she heard the bell ring over the door.

She was beginning to hate the sound.

Afraid the goon had come back, she was tempted to sneak out the back door. The goon might have been ugly, but he seemed smart enough to know he hadn't given her enough time to round up two hundred thousand dollars in the ten minutes since he had left.

Gathering the remnants of her courage, she slipped a knife into her pocket before leaving the kitchen.

She released the breath she had been unconsciously holding when she saw a teenager sitting at the counter.

"Hi," she greeted him warmly, nearly crying when the young man gave her a shy smile in return.

"Hi."

"You just get out of school?" she asked, seeing a backpack placed next to him on the chair.

"Yes, ma'am. My uncle picked me up. He had to finish

some work before taking me home. He told me I can wait here until he gets off."

"Can I get you something?"

"Yes, ma'am. I'd like a cheeseburger and some fries."

Sophie's smile broadened. "I can do that. What would you like to drink?"

"A glass of milk, ma'am."

"How about you call me Sophie, and the milk will be on the house?"

"Thank you, ma'am ..." the boy broke off with a blush.

Sophie couldn't help but laugh. "I'll let you get by with it this time, if you tell me your name."

"Logan Porter."

Sophie held out her hand. "It's nice to meet you, Logan."

"It's nice to meet you, too."

"I'll get your milk then put your hamburger on."

Reaching inside the small fridge under the condiments section, she took out the milk to pour him a large glass, then placed it down in front of him before she left him alone to return to the kitchen to put the hamburger on. Placing the fries in the basket, she waited until the hamburger was almost done before dropping the fries.

I could get the hang of this, she congratulated herself. *As long as I only have one customer at a time*, she thought wryly. Unfortunately, she wouldn't be able to pay many bills.

Dropping the fries, she readied the bun and, once it was done, placed it on the plate before pulling the fries.

When she carried the plate to the counter, she saw Logan had been drawing something in a notebook. She was able to catch a peek before it was flipped closed.

"I wish I could draw like that." Scooting the ketchup closer to him, she admitted, "I'm lucky to draw a square with a ruler."

"It's just doodling." He shrugged, staring down at his plate.

"Seemed very detailed for doodling," she remarked, looking toward the door and seeing a sheriff's deputy come swaggering inside.

The deputy appeared to look sixty with his shock of white hair until he drew closer to sit down next to Logan. Studying him up close, she subtracted about fifteen years from his age.

"Hello, may I help you?"

Logan spoke up. "This is my uncle Greer."

"Greer Porter." The deputy took his eyes off Logan's plate long enough to introduce himself.

"Nice to meet you, Deputy Porter."

"Greer will do."

"Sophie," she introduced herself.

"You Marty's kin?"

"I was his daughter."

"You know your old man was an asswipe?"

"Pretty much."

"Nothing pretty about that bastard."

Sophie was shocked at how he talked in front of the teenager.

"I can't disagree with you."

The deputy raised his eyebrows upward. "You can't?"

"No, nor do I want to. I hadn't seen my father for years before his death."

"Lucky you. He made the town miserable just for wanting to eat one of his burgers. You cook as good as he did?"

"No," she admitted.

Greer reached for the half-eaten burger on Logan's plate and took a generous bite. "Give me a couple of those bad boys and a large fry."

"What would you like to drink?"

"I'll take a milk. Might as well leave the jug—I drink a lot."

Bringing the gallon of milk to the counter with a glass, she refilled Logan's before filling Greer's.

She excused herself when she saw Greer finishing Logan's burger and went back to the kitchen. It didn't take long before she was back, placing the plates down on the counter.

"I didn't order three."

"It's for Logan, to replace the one you ate."

"I didn't order it; does that mean it's on the house?"

"Yes, if you can help me with a little problem I'm having."

The sheriff deputy squirted a glob of ketchup onto his plate. "Lady, did Logan tell you, you can bribe me with food?"

"I didn't—"

"Hush, boy." Greer scowled at his nephew before he turned his gaze back to her. "It takes more than one burger to bribe me."

"The burger wasn't meant as a bribe. I was just going to ask for some advice."

"Oh ..." Greer's expression became dejected. "What kind of advice?"

"A man come in here about an hour ago and told me my father owed him two hundred thousand dollars, and he wanted his money. Should I make a police report?"

Greer's gaze turned cunning as he took a bite. "Is the burger on the house?"

"Yes."

"Then yes, you should make the report. Do it tonight. Don't wait until morning."

Sophie started to feel scared again at the deputy's serious tone. "You think I should be worried enough to make the report today?"

"Nah, I just don't want to have to do the paperwork myself. Joel is a lazy bastard; it'll give him something to do."

She had heard of the expression dumbstruck but had never experienced it before.

Watching as the deputy ate the burger, unconcerned, while she was terrified of the man who wanted his money coming back left her speechless.

Logan, who had taken the extra burger and was eating it, placed it back down on the plate. "Uncle Greer, I think she's afraid. Maybe you should take the paperwork or tell Knox."

"She has nothing to be afraid of unless she has two hundred thousand in the safe out back." Greer picked up two fries. "Do you?"

Sophie stared at him in dismay. "Of course not."

"Then you should be good," he said, eating his fries. "Whoever he is will at least wait till morning to get the money. By then, you'll have made the report."

"I couldn't come up with that kind of money if he gave me fifty years."

"Then you have a problem." Greer started on his other burger. "Which I can help you with in the morning, or you close up when I'm done eating and mosey across the street."

Gaping at him, she couldn't believe this guy was a deputy. "Are you serious?"

"Listen up. I've been at work since six this morning. I'm tired, and when I get home, I'm going home to a house filled with youngins and their mamas expecting me to keep the little ones entertained so they can make dinner then help the older ones with their homework. If I stay late to do your paperwork, it's going to upset the balance, and I have to go home to angry women who are going to bust my chops for working late." Continuing to eat his food, he gave her a repentant stare.

"*Women*?" How had this guy found two women to live with him?

"My wife, Holly, and my brother Dustin's wife, Jessie. We share a house. Wasn't the best decision I've ever made."

Logan made a face. "It was your idea."

"Yeah, well, hindsight is foresight. I blame you on that score."

Sophie stared at them quizzingly. "How do you blame him? He's just a kid."

"He's fourteen—he's a man."

Sophie stared at the young man whom she had taken to be much younger. From Logan's red cheekbones, he must have seen how surprised she was to learn his age.

"We Porters don't show our true age," Greer said, snatching the rest of Logan's burger. "I keep telling the boy he needs to eat more protein."

She was surprised Logan was able to get any food around Greer.

Refilling his glass, Greer stared around the restaurant. "Business is slow for this time of day, huh?"

"Mostly, people just come to the door and look in," she told him. "My dad must have scared off most of his business. His lawyer told me he deliberately drove people away."

Greer made a snorting sound. "They're probably just taking a gander at you to see if you're still breathing. Two people were killed in here. I'd say that dampens their appetite."

Her stomach churned at his revelation. "Who died in here?"

"Marty and Nickel."

"God." Sophie came around to take a seat at the counter. "My dad died here?"

"Yeah. The lawyer didn't tell you?"

"No."

"Where at?" Raising a hand, she forced the bile down. "Never mind. I don't want to know."

"Logan, get her a glass of soda. It'll calm her stomach."

Logan jumped up at his uncle's order. "Here you go." He handed her a drink.

"Thanks."

Sipping the soda, she had to look away from Greer as he ate his fries.

"Who was the other man?" she asked hoarsely.

"A Last Rider named Nickel. He was a pretty good guy. They had found out Marty was using their business to transport counterfeit money. The Last Riders confronted their workers in the restaurant, and the workers pulled their guns and killed Nickel. One killed Marty when he escaped out the back door."

"His lawyer didn't tell me any of this."

"Yeah, he should have. I say the man who came here to ask for his money must have given them some for the funny money or the plates."

Sophie raised a trembling hand to her forehead. "How am I supposed to get out of this mess?" she said more to herself than Greer.

"What did he look like?"

She described the man to him.

"Sounds like an ugly son of a bitch."

"He gave me the creeps."

"I'll keep an eye out for him. If he comes back, turn the open sign upside down, and I'll come over."

"What if you're not on duty?"

Greer gave her a speculative gaze. "You hiring?"

"I'm going to be lucky to stay in business for another week."

"The customers will come back when they hear your burgers are as good as Marty's and they don't have to eat them out of a bag in the parking lot. You can't cook and take customer orders at the same time."

"You're right. I have a little money I got from tips that I could use to pay a waitress to work a few hours a day."

"Why a waitress? Why not a waiter? Logan needs a part-time job. He's wanting money to save up for a truck for when he gets old enough."

Logan turned to look at his uncle in surprise. "Dad said he was going to buy me one for my birthday."

"Dustin was going to buy a used truck. He sees you working, he might let you get a new one if you kick in some money."

Logan turned toward her. "I'm a hard worker, and I can work anytime. I'm about to get a break from school for summer."

"He ain't lying. Logan's a good boy. Besides that, whoever came here to ask for money won't lay a hand on you when he's here."

Sophie shook her head. "I don't want to take a chance that Logan could get hurt."

Greer laughed. "No one in town is stupid enough to touch a hair on Logan's head."

Her eyes widened at Greer laughing. "Why not?"

"Because the motherfucker would be dead."

Chapter Eleven

J ody checked to make sure his new shirt was still tucked
into his jeans.

"You look fine," Ginny assured him as they walked
toward the diner.

"I need to look better than fine. I have a lot of ground to
make up for. I need to knock her socks off."

"You will."

Jody wasn't as certain as Ginny was.

Nervous, he opened the door to the diner and saw two
customers sitting at a table. At least he was assured she was still
giving the restaurant a go.

"Have a seat. I'll be right with you."

Ginny and he stared at each other at the female shout
coming from the kitchen.

They went to a booth and sat down, Jody sitting on the
side where he could see the front of the restaurant.

They didn't have to wait long before Sophie came in from
the back, carrying two plates. After she set the plates down in
front of the other two customers, she approached their table.

Jody noticed the smile she directed at Ginny didn't include him.

"Hello, how are you today?"

"Good." Ginny smiled back at her.

It was obvious Sophie was taken aback.

"You're Silas' sister?"

Ginny nodded.

She stared at Ginny a moment longer, it looked as if she thought Ginny was familiar but in the end she couldn't place her.

"Silas said you used to work here."

"I did." Her expression turned morose. "I was also a friend of your father's. I'm sorry for your loss."

"Don't be. We weren't close."

Ginny didn't seem shocked at Sophie's response. "I understand. Just because he befriended me doesn't make him a good father to you."

Jody saw the sadness on his sister's face. She had been deeply hurt when she found out about the crimes Marty had committed.

Ginny gave a slight shake of her head. "Are you enjoying the restaurant?"

Sophie made a face. "It certainly is not as easy as I thought it would be. I would have listed the restaurant for sale already if your brothers hadn't come in. Their tip allowed me enough money to stay in business for the rest of the week. You and your brother make my fifth and six customers this morning, so I guess business is picking up slowly. I had to fire George yesterday, so I've had to shorten the menu to a few menu items I can cook."

"Jody said your father and mother will be able to help when they get here in a couple of weeks."

She nodded. "If I make it that long."

"You will. I can help. I know how to make most of the old menu. I can help you out until your parents get here."

"I can help, too," Jody offered.

"That's okay. I wouldn't be able to pay you. I hired Logan Porter to work a few hours a day in the afternoons."

"Good, then you're set. I'll help you out a few hours in the morning, and Jody can come in during the lunch rush."

"What lunch rush?" Sophie gave a lackluster laugh. "I'm only getting a couple of customers every few hours."

"The customers will pick up. Once I teach you how to cook a couple of dishes on the menu, people will have to make reservations to come in here."

"Which ones?"

"The cardiac special."

"The cardiac special?"

"Country fried ham with red-eye gravy, fried potatoes, two fried eggs, and biscuits," Ginny told her. "They also loved the fried chicken special with soup, beans, and cornbread. I also can help you get your hands on some venison sausage. You fry that up with some scrambled eggs, onions, and peppers, then wrap it up like a burrito, and they will sell out before you can say Hallelujah!"

Sophie burst out laughing. "You can teach me how to cook everything you just mentioned?"

"I can teach you how to cook it in your sleep." Ginny grinned.

"I can't accept your help without paying you."

Ginny gave her a considering look. "Are you allergic to goats?"

"Not as far as I know."

"I have a few goats that need to be milked daily. When your parents get here, you could spend an hour a day milking the goats for me until you pay off the hours I work here."

Sophie's gaze switched to his.

"After you pay off Ginny's hours, you can pay off mine ... I hate goats."

"I can do that."

"I would think it over. Those goats are a pain in the ass."

"I worked in a cafeteria for a nursing home before moving here. I could tell you horror stories about what I had to deal with."

Ginny and Jody both grimaced.

"I can imagine," he said as the door opened, sending the bell tingling.

A woman entered, looking around the restaurant until she sighted him. "Hey, Jody!" she gushed, coming toward their table. "You come into town for lunch?"

Jody groaned inwardly. Could he catch a fucking break?

"Hey, Mina," he responded with a tight smile.

"I'm on my lunch hour; you mind if I join you?"

Before he could say anything, Mina squeezed herself into the small portion of the booth seat he was sitting on.

He didn't know what to do. The last thing he needed was to come across as being an asshole two days in a row, but he didn't have an easy way of getting rid of her, either.

Ginny saved him. Sliding out of the booth, she hooked her arm around Sophie's. "How about we check on your customers? Then we can go into the kitchen and see what we have to work with."

"She didn't take our order," Mina complained.

"What do you want, and I'll go tell them?"

Mina gave him a sultry wink. "What I want, I can't have here. You want to go to my house, and I'll make you something to eat?"

"No, thanks. I won't be coming by your house anymore. I'm seeing someone."

"Since when has that stopped you?"

Jody removed the hand that had moved to his thigh.

Looking up, he realized Ginny and Sophie were able to see what Mina had done under the table.

"What do you want to order?" Jody asked through tight lips.

Mina pouted at him. "What's with the cold shoulder?"

"I told you I'm seeing someone."

Mina straightened away from him. "Like in, you're really dating someone?"

"Not yet. I'm working on it. Currently, our relationship is in the talking stage."

Her expression turned relieved. "That's okay, then. I can take care of you until you get past the talking stage."

"No. I plan to be faithful to her."

"Jody Coleman"—Mina giggled, scraping his nerves—"you don't have a faithful bone in your body."

"I do now."

Mina rolled her eyes at him and got out of the booth. She placed her palms on the table, giving him a generous view of her chest. "When you get tired of sweet-talking her, call me— you know my number. I promise you'll get more out of me than talking."

Jody wanted to bury his face in his hands as she sashayed out of the restaurant. Thankfully, Ginny and Sophie had gone to the kitchen.

They were still in there when the customers got up to stand by the register.

"Hey, Tate, Dustin; how are you doing?"

Tate nodded his head and lay money down on top of their ticket. "I heard you and Ginny are going to be helping out Sophie. Logan's going to be working here after school."

"So I heard," Jody told the two brothers.

"You hear one of Marty's buddies stopped by yesterday?"

"Yeah." Jody lowered his voice. "Greer called Silas last night. We'll keep an eye out."

"You won't be the only one." Tate's craggy face was set to no-nonsense. "We'll do what we can to help her make a go of this place, but if anything happens to Logan, kin or not, blood will be spilled, regardless of who gets in the way."

Jody didn't look away from Tate's gaze. "Understood." Jody mimicked Tate's hard gaze. "And so you understand, my happiness isn't the only one that rides on Sophie staying in town."

Chapter Twelve

"You've made a good start. The kitchen is spotless. It was always a mess when I worked here."

Sophie stared around the kitchen proudly. "I worked in restaurants most of my life. My mother taught me to keep everything clean. To be honest, I knew if this kitchen wasn't spotless when she got here, she'd give me hell."

"I bet you can't wait for your parents to arrive."

Sophie nodded. "I'm looking forward to us not being bossed around. That's why this restaurant means so much to me. My parents have had it rough since Mom's divorce from Marty. He made their lives a living hell. They've had to move from one state to another to get away from him."

"You moved with them?"

"Yes. I wanted to be close by if they needed me."

"I understand. I'm close to my family, too."

"Your family is really nice. If not for the tip they gave me yesterday, I was about to call a realtor. I don't want my parents moving here only to find themselves jobless."

"We're going to make sure that doesn't happen."

She tilted her head to watch Ginny's reaction. "Why?"

"The town has missed having a place to hang out. We've missed the food, coming to eat here after church. It's been depressing to see the diner closed."

"People aren't exactly rushing in like they missed it being open."

"They're skittish. They'll slowly come back, and when they do, they'll stay loyal customers."

As they talked, they heard the bell ring.

"I should check and see if I have a customer." She started for the door.

"Don't worry. If someone came in, Jody would have told you."

As Sophie showed her the food supply she'd purchased, Ginny took out her cell phone to write a list of the items they would need to prepare the dishes she wanted to teach her. When they were done, Ginny texted her the list.

Sophie stared at it in dismay. "Can we just start with a couple of the dishes? I'm afraid I don't have enough money to purchase all of them."

"Let me worry about that. It's not like you can get away to do any shopping. I'll send Jody to buy what we need. You can pay me back when the restaurant is making more money."

Sophie shook her head. "Thank you, but I can't accept that kind of help. Besides, Jody might have plans for the rest of the day. I'll go to the store after I close."

"Jody won't mind. He's off today."

"I'm sure he'd rather be spending time with his new girlfriend."

Ginny seemed confused. "What new girlfriend? He's never had a girlfriend."

Had she unintentionally told Ginny a secret Jody hadn't wanted to share?

"I must be mistaken."

Ginny nodded, her frown clearing. "You must be. Jody is

waiting for his soul mate. He's never even been on a date, as far as I know."

Sophie could only stare at her. Poor woman was disillusioned where Jody was concerned.

"Soul mate?"

"Oh, yes, all my brothers are waiting for theirs. Well, except for Matthew—he found his," Ginny explained.

"Really?" It was everything Sophie could do not to laugh.

Ginny must have read the laughter in her eyes, though. "You don't believe me?"

"Jody told you that?"

"All my brothers know they have soul mates."

"Are they faithful to their soul mates?"

Ginny grimaced. "I'm not making excuses—I don't want you to think I am—*but* a few of my brothers may have the philosophy that, until they actually meet their soul mates, it's not really cheating."

"Isn't that convenient?"

Ginny winced at her sarcastic tone. "Silas and I warned them that their soul mates won't see it the same way. You have to understand that, to them, they've known about their soul mates since they were children. It's like being promised to go on a magical trip to this magical place and having to wait. After so long, they get tired of waiting, and they take small excursions to different places."

"I see." She didn't, yet she didn't want to hurt Ginny's feelings by telling her one of her brothers—from what she could tell—hadn't gone on small excursions. He made regular trips.

"Do you believe in soul mates?"

Sophie had to think about it for a minute. Did she believe in soul mates?

"I think couples can be deeply in love enough to believe they're soul mates. Do I personally believe they are? No. No one knows who their soul mate can really be. Does that mean every woman or man they've been with is their soul mate, and then, when the relationship ends, they say I guess they weren't their soul mate? It gives them an excuse to give up on a relationship."

Wondering at the strange expression Ginny made, she laughed. "You're married." Sophie looked at the wedding rings on Ginny's hand. "Are you married to your soul mate?"

"Yes."

"Then I'm glad you found him. Did you know he was your soul mate before you were together?" Sophie was about to prove her point.

"I did."

Sophie blinked at her. "Okay ..." she drawled out. "But that was after you started dating."

"Before."

"How did you know he was your soul mate?"

"I saw his face. The moment I saw him, I knew he was my soul mate."

Sophie had another word for what Ginny probably thought happened. *Lust.* With Treepoint being a small town, her parents would have drummed into her to save herself for marriage. She hadn't been particularly adventuresome in the bedroom herself, but just because she had found a man earth-shakingly attractive, like Jody, she wasn't going to chalk those feelings up to finding her soul mate. If he was her soul mate, she thought sarcastically, she would be crying, right after she kicked him in his balls a couple of times.

"I'm happy you found yours, but I won't hold my breath about finding mine."

Ginny seemed about to say something then changed her mind.

Sophie thought Ginny was thinking of a way to change

her mind about soul mates. She was going to make it easy for her.

"I'm not ruling out having a soul mate. I have my eye on a man I've met."

Ginny's face lightened. "You have?" she asked her happily.

"I have. I just need to ask if he is dating someone before I make my move."

"Who is he?"

"Isaac."

Chapter Thirteen

"I think that went well. Don't you?" Jody asked as they got back in the truck after spending most of the morning helping Sophie out at the diner.

"Umm ... I guess."

Jody turned to look at Ginny once he was driving on the road back to their homes. "What does that mean?"

"It means, your goose may be cooked. She doesn't believe in soul mates, which Gavin didn't either when I told him, so I'm sure you'll be able to convince her. On the other hand, you might not want to."

"How in the hell did you get on the subject of soul mates?"

"I really don't remember. She noticed the way Mina acted around you, and she thought you two were dating."

His hands tightened on the steering wheel. More than one of his chickens had come home to roost.

"Go on," he said through tight lips.

"I told her how none of you have ever been on a date because you're waiting for your soul mates."

"I don't want her thinking I'm a nerd."

"Oh ... umm ... I don't think she thinks you're a nerd from the way Mina came on to you."

"Does she believe in soul mates?"

"Not exactly."

"What in the hell does that mean?"

"It means she thinks that if men believe in soul mates, it only gives them an excuse to break off relationships when they don't work out. She said that, so how do you think she's going to react when she finds out you knew who your soul mate is and had sex with half the female population in town?"

"I haven't had sex with half of the women in town."

"I'm sorry," she apologized. "With all the women in your age range," she clarified.

"Dammit," he growled.

"You brought this on yourself. The good news is I think she'll be staying, and I may have convinced her about soul mates."

"At least that's good."

"The bad news is she's kind of interested in Issac."

His jaw tautened. "She's not Issac's soul mate. She's mine."

"I'm not the one you have to convince."

"I will," he said determinedly.

"You're going to have an uphill battle," she warned.

"Then I guess it'll have to be."

"I think I know exactly where you should make your first move."

Jody pushed the cart around the grocery store, looking for Sophie. Placing a box of Captain Crunch in the cart, he went down another aisle. Where was she? He had seen her car outside.

When he turned down another aisle, he spotted her at a frozen food freezer.

Casually opening a freezer door, he took out a bag of chicken nuggets before wheeling his cart toward Sophie.

"Hey, there," he greeted her when she turned her head at hearing the clanking cart.

"Hello," she said, then turned back to the freezer.

"Having trouble finding something?"

"No, just deciding which hashbrowns to get."

"Shredded," he advised. "That way, you can add onions and peppers."

She didn't look at him. "They make them with peppers and onions already added."

"Are they for you personally or the restaurant?"

"The restaurant."

"Then go for the ones without them. Fresh is always better."

"The hashbrowns aren't fresh."

"Yeah, but the onions and peppers will make people think they are if you cook them on the grill."

Sophie opened the door of the freezer and took out several bags, then started rolling her cart away.

Jody rolled his behind her.

"How were things after Ginny and I left? Did business pick up?"

"No." Rolling her cart to the meat department, she stared around before turning toward him. "Do you know where fatback is? I don't know what it looks like, so I wouldn't recognize it if I saw it."

"I'll show you." He pointed to the meat cooler with bacon. "Fatback is over there."

Heading over, he picked up several blocks to show her. "This is it."

Sophie stared at them before taking them from him. "Thank you. I would have never found them."

"You're welcome."

She wheeled her cart away, but he followed her.

"Ginny said she had a good time working at the restaurant. I think she gets bored staying at home all the time."

"I like Ginny. She's really nice."

Jody had to hold back his laughter. "You've never seen her mad. When she is, you have to watch yourself. She believes in superstitions, and her paybacks are very creative."

"That's understandable. With as many brothers as she has, she needs to keep the element of surprise."

"Once—"

"I'm sorry," she cut him off, "but I need to finish shopping so I can get home. It's been a long day."

"Oh ... okay. I'll see you tomorrow."

"Bye."

Jody wheeled his cart down an aisle as she went toward the dairy section. He was becoming disheartened. His soul mate couldn't stand him, and he didn't know how to regroup. She would come around, right? They *were* soul mates. She had to at least be attracted to him. He knew he was by his body's reaction to her. His star was aligned with hers in the sky; he had seen it for himself.

Jealousy still burned that Sophie had asked Ginny if Issac was dating anyone. He wasn't used to being jealous of his brothers.

He made a sound under his breath. If she had a bad opinion of him, Issac was way worse.

He went up the cookie aisle so he could keep his eyes on the checkout aisle. He had picked out a couple boxes when he saw Sophie getting in line. Pulling his cart behind her, he waited to check out.

She hadn't gotten as much as he'd thought she would. He

remembered Ginny telling him she refused to let him shop for her because she didn't want to borrow the money, so it was everything he could do not to tell her to turn her cart around and get what she needed.

He memorized the items she had bought as the checker bagged the groceries for her and wanted to disappear when the cashier turned a bright red and dropped the loaf of bread she had been about to bag.

"Sorry," Betsy apologized to Sophie before turning a flirtatious glance on him. "Hi, Jody. I didn't see you come in the store. What's up?"

"Nothing, just doing a little shopping," he answered, wanting to back his cart out of the checkout lane.

Betsy picked up one of the bags of hashbrowns, holding it mid-air instead of bagging it as she continued talking with him. "I haven't seen you since I dropped off those muffins I made for you."

"Been busy," he muttered, pointedly eyeing the hashbrowns.

"Oh ..." Betsy turned redder. "Sorry."

Plopping the hashbrowns in the bag, she quickly bagged the rest of Sophie's groceries. He didn't miss the disdainful way Sophie looked at him as she headed toward the door

He put up his groceries on the counter.

"I can make you some more if you want?" Betsy offered.

"No, thanks. I'm on a diet."

She eyed him as she ran a pack of Oreos over the scanner.

"Those are for Jacob." He hastily told her, taking out his wallet. He wanted to tell her to hurry as Betsy took her time and started bagging his groceries himself.

"I'll do that."

"I'm in a hurry. Jacob is waiting for me to get home."

Giving him a disappointed glance, she took the cash he handed her. "Call me ..."

Jody picked up his groceries before she could continue.

Outside, he saw Sophie's taillights as she pulled out of the parking lot.

"Damn it to hell," he lamented about his luck as he put the groceries in his truck.

The last thing he wanted to do was go back inside the store, but he also wanted Sophie to have what she needed. So, he went back through the store and picked up what was on the list that she hadn't purchased.

Without a doubt, she was going to be angry that he had bought the items, but he had already thought of a way to circumvent her. She might refuse them from him, but Ginny had a way of talking anyone into doing what she wanted. She had nabbed Reaper, and that son of bitch hadn't known what had hit him.

Had she used some superstitious crap to make Reaper fall for her? He wouldn't put anything past her.

When he got home, he was going to call Ginny. He wasn't above playing unfair to get his soul mate, especially when she already had her eye on Isaac. His dad had always told him everything was fair in love and war.

Chapter Fourteen

Was there any woman in town who wasn't attracted to Jody as if he were catnip? Slamming the trunk of her car closed, she carried her groceries into her apartment building, then used her elbow to push the elevator button. Her blood still boiled at the way the cashier had acted.

Why do you care? she asked herself, stepping into the elevator when it opened.

Using her elbow again to press her floor button, she told herself she didn't care. It was just embarrassing for womankind with the way they acted.

Yeah, right. She laughed grimly at herself. *As if you didn't practically orgasm when you saw Jody for the first time.*

That was before she realized what a hound dog he was, she consoled herself. She hadn't let him know, either. She would rather die a torturous death than let that lover boy know she had fallen victim to the pheromones he was using to set women's crotches on fire. She bet he used his hot-as-hell body to chase after women. Then, when they gave in, he dropped them like a hot potato.

She was still mentally griping about Jody when she stepped off the elevator and walked down the hall to her apartment. As she bent down to set one of the grocery bags on the floor to unlock her door, her eyes automatically went to the doorknob. Her breath caught in her throat at seeing the door wasn't closed all the way.

Setting the other bag down, she pushed the door open. Gasping at the destruction she encountered in her apartment, she reached into her purse for her phone to call 911.

After telling the dispatcher that her apartment had been broken into, she heard the shock in the woman's voice.

"Stay outside your apartment. I'll send a deputy right over."

"Thank you." Shaken, it took two tries to end the call.

What if the burglar was still inside? Should she go back downstairs and wait there?

Leaving the groceries, she moved away from her door to stand by the elevator. She stood there anxiously, waiting for the police to arrive. If anyone came out of her apartment, she planned to scream bloody murder.

The elevator door opening had her jumping back. When she recognized the deputy walking out of the elevator, she was about to throw herself into his arms but thankfully caught herself before she did.

"Deputy Bevere." The deputy had taken her report about the man who had come into the restaurant wanting money. His concerned face eased some of her anxiety now that he was here.

"What's going on?"

"When I came home, my apartment door was unlocked. When I pushed the door open, I saw my living room has been ransacked."

"Did you go inside?"

"No, I was too afraid."

"Which apartment is it?"

Sophie pointed down the hall. "I left the door open."

"You stay here while I check it out," he ordered, removing his gun from his holster. Deputy Bevere was scary looking, even before he pulled his gun, wearing his hair short in a military style that accented the broad planes of his face.

Sophie watched as he walked down the hallway then went into her apartment. Nervous, she waited for him to come back out. Biting her lip, she gripped her phone in case she needed to call 911 again. Shouldn't he have backup?

When he didn't immediately come back out, her tension increased. Then she was relieved when he did to nod to her.

As she walked down the hall, she kept her gaze trained on him, expecting the burglar to tackle him down. *Get a grip*, she told herself as she came up to him.

"The apartment is empty. Whoever it was did a number on the place."

Reluctantly, she turned to look inside her apartment. "I saw the living room when I opened the door."

"Your bedroom and bathroom are worse."

"Great." Almost in tears, she started to step into her apartment to see the damage for herself.

"I need for you to stay here. The sheriff is on his way, with a lab technician. Your apartment is going to have to be dusted for prints, as well as have pictures taken."

Sophie stared at the destroyed mess inside her apartment and saw it for what it was—the straw that broke the camel's back. She was done. There was no way she would have her mother and father come to Treepoint.

The burglar hadn't been content to destroy what was lying around her apartment; they had ripped open boxes that she had yet to unpack.

Heartsick at seeing her childhood photos smashed on floor, she turned away to lean against the wall.

"Do you think the man who wanted the money Marty owed him did this?"

The deputy gave her a sympathetic glance. "That's not a wild guess. I'd say it more than likely was. This is the first burglary in the last two years. He could have been looking for something you had that belonged to Marty."

"I don't have—"

"Sophie."

Sophie turned at hearing Ginny's voice. Both Ginny and Jody were coming down the hall. When Ginny reached her, she pulled her into her arms.

"What happened?" Ginny asked softly.

"Someone broke into my apartment. They broke my pictures ... I don't understand why they broke my pictures."

"Could be a threatening tactic," Deputy Bevere said grimly.

"Why would someone be threatening her?" Jody asked.

When the deputy remained silent, Sophie told them, "A man came into the restaurant a couple of days ago, asking for the money Marty owed him."

"How much?" Ginny's armed tightened around her proactively.

"Two hundred thousand."

Raising her head from Ginny's shoulder, she looked up and found Jody's face. Dismayed at the formidable expression on it, she turned back to Ginny's. "I'm okay now."

"Are you sure?" Ginny released her but remained close to her side.

"How did you find out?"

"I was still in town when I heard you had been robbed. It came over the scanner in my truck. I called Ginny—she was visiting some friends not far from here."

Jody stepped around them to look inside her apartment.

"They had a field day, didn't they?" Stony-faced, he moved away from the door.

"The deputy said the sheriff is on his way, and a technician. I can't go inside to put my groceries away."

Ginny patted her on her arm. "It's going to take a few hours for them to get the evidence they need. Come home with me and stay the night."

"I don't want to impose—"

"You should go with Ginny," the deputy advised. "There's no need for you to stay here to watch. When you get up in the morning, we need to do a walkthrough so we can make a list of your missing items."

"I have a spare bedroom; you won't be any trouble." Ginny bent down to pick up the grocery bag. "Let's go. I'm not taking no for an answer."

"I'm too tired to argue. Besides, I don't think I would get any sleep if I did stay here tonight."

Ginny looked at Jody. "Are you coming?"

Jody shook his head. "No, you go ahead. I'm going to wait for Knox."

Sophie took another glance at Jody, still shocked at how scary he looked. She had taken him for a good-looking guy, only concerned about having a good time. By the way he looked now, she had underestimated him.

The bugler had done her a favor by showing her that Jody could be a force to be reckoned with.

Chapter Fifteen

J ody remained silent until the women were enclosed in the elevator. Then his eyes slid back to the destruction that had taken place.

"You think the person who wanted the money did the break-in?"

"We haven't had a break-in in two years. I don't recognize anyone in town fitting the description Sophie gave me. Do you?"

"No." Greer had given the physical description to Silas, which he had shared with the rest of the family. "He'd be hard to mix up with the way she described him."

"Makes sense it was him, then. Sophie is new in town; who else would break in to do this type of damage?"

"I can think of someone," Jodie said grimly, seeing the sheriff and another deputy carrying a case getting off the elevator.

"Jody."

"Knox," Jody greeted the sheriff.

"What are you doing here?"

"Sophie is a friend of mine."

At the explanation, Knox turned to Deputy Bevere. "Fill me in."

The deputy did, finishing by telling Knox that Jody had an idea of someone else who could have broken in.

"Leland, go ahead and get started taking prints," Knox told the deputy carrying the case before turning his attention back to Jody.

"Okay, Jody, who do you think is responsible for this?"

"I can't be sure. I need to talk to her first."

Knox looked inside the apartment. "A jealous rage?" Knox nodded. "I wouldn't be surprised. I had to issue tickets to two of your side pieces six months ago, coming out of the gym, for disorderly contact."

"I wasn't aware of that. Who were they?"

"Baylin and Amber."

"I had no idea."

"Who do you think wrecked Sophie's apartment?"

"Baylin." Jody tilted his head to the side. "She lives next door."

Joel Bevere gave him thumbs-up. "That's convenient."

Jody gave him a dirty look.

Joel cleared his throat. "I meant for Baylin."

"I'll have to wait and see if we find any fingerprints and ask Sophie if anything is stolen before I can get a warrant for her fingerprints and to search her apartment."

"*You* may have to wait, but *I* don't." Jody strode toward the apartment next door.

"Jody, wait," Knox called out to him.

"Don't you find it strange that no one else has come out of their apartment?" Jody arched a brow at him.

Knox nodded. "Let me handle it."

"How about you let me handle it? It's my mess to clean up."

Before Knox could stop him, he knocked on the door.

A couple of minutes went by before he heard the sound of Baylin unlocking her door.

"Jody!" She took a step into the hallway to put her arms around his neck. "If I knew you were coming by, I would have put on your favorite nightie."

His hands went to her wrists to pull her away from him. "I didn't come by here to see you. I came to check on Sophie. Someone broke into her apartment."

A vindictive glint appeared in her eyes. "If you're expecting me to feel bad for her, you knocked on the wrong door."

"Why wouldn't you feel bad for her? She hasn't done anything to you."

Baylin gave a careless shrug. "I couldn't care less about her, one way or another."

"I figured you would be upset, with you living next door to her."

"Why would I be upset? I've been home all day. Anyone brave enough to break into my place won't go out the same way he went in."

"So, you were here all day?" Knox asked, silently walking up to them.

Baylin turned startled eyes toward Knox. "Yes," she answered slowly. "Today's my off day."

"You didn't hear any noise from next door?"

Her eyes went from Knox to his. "Not a sound. I really can't hear anything from her apartment."

"That's not true. When Gloria lived there, you complained every time I was here about how much noise she makes."

"Sophie is much quieter."

Jody knew the bitch was lying. The vindictive glint in her eyes had disappeared to be replaced with fear.

Knox noticed something he hadn't.

"How did you get that gash on your forearm?"

Baylin tugged the arm of her housecoat down, which had slid up when she placed her arms around his neck. "I broke a glass in the garbage disposal," she told Knox timidly.

"Baylin, I'm going to go back to check the apartment out. If I find any blood, I'll be back with a warrant to get a blood sample from you."

Baylin watched Knox until he went inside the apartment. Then, grabbing Jody by the arm, she tugged him inside her apartment and closed the door. "You have to help me," she pleaded with him with frightened eyes.

Jody crossed his arms over his chest. "Why should you be afraid? Is Knox going to find your blood inside?"

"You bastard, you know I did it. You have to help me."

"Why should I?" His stony expression took in her appearance. "There was no reason for you to trash Sophie's apartment."

"My friend saw you in her restaurant today, working behind the counter. It didn't take you long to replace me."

His arms went out to her shoulders. "Sophie didn't replace you. We were never in a relationship. Get that through your head."

"We will be. You just need time to figure out how much you care about me."

"I used to like you, Baylin. We had some good times. I don't need more time to figure out what you mean to me. You mean *nothing* to me," he told her coldly.

Her face went ashen. "You don't mean that." She started pressing herself against him, trying to kiss him.

"Cut it out." Jody stepped away from her reach. "My advice is to tell Knox what you did before he has to get a warrant. You might be able to keep it quiet until it goes to court."

"I'll lose my job at the hospital if anyone finds out about this."

"You should have thought about that before wrecking Sophie's apartment," he told her ruthlessly.

"I just wanted her to leave town."

Jody stared at her pitilessly. "I can't believe I misjudged you so badly. I could never be with a woman who would deliberately hurt another person."

"You don't have a problem hurting me!"

"If I hurt you, you should have taken that out on me, not blindsided someone else who was nice to you. That's fucked up."

"I'll talk to her." Baylin's voice turned shrill. "I'll pay for the damages."

Jody reached out to take her by the jaw, controlling his strength so he wouldn't hurt her. "You don't go near Sophie, or the next time, the only one leaving town will be you. You let Knox do the talking for you. If you're lucky, Sophie will let it drop. If not, you accept the punishment. Personally, I prefer they lock your ass up in jail." Releasing her, he turned for the door.

"You don't mean that!"

"Yes, I do. You came after someone who belongs to me. Make no mistake, Baylin; I protect those who belong to me, and Sophie belongs to me." Jody pinned her in place with his stare. "I better not find out you're part of the reason customers aren't coming into the diner because you're bad-mouthing her."

When she shifted her gaze away from his, Jody knew he had hit the nail on the head.

"You're a piece of work. You better fix this mess you created, or so help me, I will."

"I'll fix it." Her hand went to her mouth as she started crying.

Jody turned to open the door, motioning for her to go through. "I'd start now."

Chapter Sixteen

Looking at her watch, Sophie dragged herself out of bed then lay back down. She pulled the pillow over her face and started crying, smothering her tears in the pillow, wishing her mother were there instead.

After a good cry, she forced herself out of bed and went to the bathroom attached to the bedroom Ginny had given her last night. Turning on the faucet, she splashed cold water on her face. Then, after wiping off her face with a hand towel, she grimaced at her puffy eyes.

She walked back into the bedroom to dress in the jeans and sweatshirt Ginny had loaned her. The jeans were too tight, but the sweatshirt was long enough to hide the gaping space. With lagging footsteps, she left the bedroom, hoping to leave the house without seeing Ginny. Still on the verge of more tears, she didn't think she would be able to handle any sympathy without breaking down.

"Good morning," Ginny greeted her cheerfully, coming out of the kitchen. "How are you doing?"

"Better. Thank you."

"I just made a pot of coffee. Would you like a cup before you head to the diner?"

"No, thanks. I'm not going to the diner."

"Oh ... then you're going to your apartment. Give me a couple of minutes to get dressed, and I'll go with you."

Sophie shook her head. "I'm not going to my apartment, at least not yet. I'm going to a realty company. I'm going to sell the diner."

"I'd say I'm surprised, but I'm not. Since you're not opening the diner, stay for a cup of coffee. I can refer a realtor to you who will try to get you the best price. Drake doesn't open his office for a couple of hours."

"I could use a cup of coffee."

Sophie took a seat at the table next to the kitchen while Ginny got the coffee. She noticed several missed calls from Knox. She would call him back after she drank the coffee, sure he was going to ask her to go back to the apartment to see if anything was stolen. She would need to drink a whole pot laced with Baileys before she worked up enough courage to go there.

"Here you go." Ginny sat down across from her.

Sophie eyed her. "If you're going to convince me not to sell the diner, don't. I'm more than ready to leave Treepoint."

"Are you just as ready to give up your dreams?"

"I can buy another restaurant in another town."

"If you do sell the restaurant, where would you buy another one?"

"I don't know. I guess I'll use Google to find out where restaurants are for sale and start looking there."

"In a new town you haven't been before?"

"Yes."

"You could run into the same difficulties there you have here. Sometimes when you move to a new place, it takes time to fit in."

"I don't need my parents coming to Treepoint to be unhappy. This is supposed to be our new beginning."

"Sophie"—Ginny stared at her earnestly—"Treepoint can be your and your parents' new beginning. I'm very happy, but not too long ago, I was miserable, thinking it would be better if I just ran away and disappeared. If not for Gavin coming after me, I wouldn't have the life I live now. You don't have to give up; you have more support here than you know."

"I can't expect you all to keep helping me. You've just met me."

Ginny's hand moved across the table to rest on hers. "I have a sixth sense about people. When I met you, I felt as if we would become good friends."

Sophie had to admit to having the same feeling, yet she didn't tell Ginny that. It wouldn't do any good to deepen their friendship when she would be leaving.

"My whole family will be upset if you leave."

"Your family has been very kind to me."

"Just give it another few days. Talk to Drake and find out how much you would make from the sale. I just don't want you to give up before you explore all your options."

Sighing, she took a sip of her coffee. "I'll talk to your friend, then come to a decision."

"Great. I really want you to stay."

A knock at Ginny's door had both of them looking toward it.

"Come in!" Ginny yelled out, and Jody opened the door.

Laughing at Sophie's startled expression, Ginny got up from the table. "I knew it was Jody," she explained. "I texted him when I was in the kitchen. He wanted to talk to you before you left." Ginny turned to go into the kitchen. "I'll get you some coffee, Jody," she said from over her shoulder.

"Thanks, sis." Jody pulled out a chair next to where Ginny

had been sitting. "I wanted to talk to you before you left. Have you talked to Knox yet?"

Sophie grimaced. "No, I haven't returned his calls."

Ginny handed Jody his coffee. "I need to start a load of clothes. I'll be right back."

Sophie suspiciously watched Ginny leave before returning her gaze to Jody. "Is something going on I don't know about?"

"The sheriff discovered who broke into your apartment and needs to know what you want to do."

Surprised at how quickly the sheriff had apprehended the burglar, she felt a wave of relief flow through her.

"Was it the man who wanted the money Marty owed him?"

"No. It was your neighbor. Baylin."

Her mouth dropped open. "Come again?"

"Baylin, the woman who lives next to you, is the person who trashed your apartment."

"Tell me you're kidding?"

"I wish I could," he said flatly.

"Your ex-girlfriend? That's who we're talking about?"

"Never a girlfriend, but ... unfortunately, yes."

"Did she say what she wanted to steal?"

"She didn't steal anything. At least, that's what she said. We won't know for sure until you go back to your apartment and go through your things."

"If she didn't want to steal anything, then why did she break into my apartment?"

Jody stared at her steadily. "She was jealous of you and wanted you to leave town. I'm afraid that's not all. She's been talking shit about the restaurant to her coworkers and friends. That's part of the reason your business has been so slow."

"But why?" Why had Baylin gone after her like that? She had thought she was nice when she met her at the diner.

"She is jealous of you."

Sophie sat back in her chair, astounded. "She's jealous of me? You're kidding."

"No, I wouldn't joke about something like this."

"There's no way Baylin is jealous of me. She's gorgeous."

"That's a matter of opinion."

She gave him a baleful look. "You know she's gorgeous; why are you acting like she isn't?"

"I didn't say she wasn't, only that Baylin is jealous of you."

"Why would she be jealous of me? I don't see her being jealous of me owning the diner or my apartment."

"She wasn't jealous of either of those things."

"Then what?"

"She knows I am attracted to you."

Sophie felt the heat pour into her face.

"You're not disregarding that possibility like you did the others?"

She stared down at her neatly trimmed fingernails. "Nothing like a woman being scorned to bring out the claws."

"Despite what you believe, I wasn't in a relationship with Baylin."

"I heard you and Baylin in her apartment. Try again."

"We hooked up, that's it," he said firmly.

"She thought otherwise."

"I know, and I'm sorry. I never led Baylin on. She always came on to me, and I told her loud and clear that I didn't want a relationship with her."

"Spending six hours in her bed with you must have given her other ideas."

"I get that it was in her head, but other than tattooing it on my dick, I couldn't have made it plainer to her."

Sophie gaped at him before snapping her mouth closed. "Or, if you knew she was taking your hookups to mean something more, you could have kept your little friend zipped in."

Jody burst into laughter.

Her hand tightened on her coffee cup.

His eyes dropped to her white-knuckled grip on the cup. "I wouldn't," he warned.

She loosened her grip. "I don't know what you mean." She glowered at him.

"Yeah, you do, but I'll let it pass for now. It's getting a little heated in here, and I don't want to give you another reason to run, so I suggest you call Knox and hear what he has to say."

Latching on to the excuse to avoid talking to him any further, she called the sheriff. She was still talking to him when Ginny walked back into the room to sit down at the table. When she ended the call, she looked at the brother and sister. "The sheriff gave me the option to press charges on Baylin. She's offered to pay for any damages."

Ginny gave her a commiserating glance. "What are you going to do?"

Chapter Seventeen

"I don't know what to do. I don't want her to go to jail, which I guess settles it. I'm just going to sell the diner and move away."

"What does you dropping the charges have to do with you having to move away?" Jody's jaw clenched.

"I certainly don't want to live next door to her or in the same building."

"I can't blame her there." Ginny looked at her brother, nodding her head.

Jody nodded back. "There is another option, one that I think will be much safer and more convenient for you, anyway."

Sophie looked at Jody. "Such as?"

"We have an empty trailer here you can live in. It's not very large, but it's comfortable. Also, once you start milking the goats for us, you'll already be here. You could milk them before you go to work in the morning. It would be a fair exchange."

"How would it be a fair exchange? Milking a few goats isn't going to be worth the rent of a trailer."

"The trailer is just sitting empty. We wouldn't have to worry about any animals making a home inside."

Sophie bit her lip. The offer was tempting. She hated living in the apartment without any yard of her own.

"At first, you thought the man whom Marty owes money was the one who broke into your apartment. Obviously, he frightened you. You wouldn't have to worry about that if you lived here. No one steps on our property unless we know about it."

Ginny took over convincing her when Jody stopped. "When your parents come to town, they can take over the apartment for you … unless you were planning on living with them."

"I don't think the trailer would be big enough for all of you to live in," Jody hastened to add.

"I wasn't going to live with them. I was going to find another apartment when they moved to town."

"This would save you a lot of money from renting another place, especially with the diner just starting out."

"True. That is … if I decide to stay."

"You haven't given the diner a chance. Are you sure you even want to own a restaurant?"

Giving Jody a hostile glance, she stuck her chin out stubbornly. "I'm sure. The problem is I should have looked before I leaped. I don't have enough capital to make it until it thrives. When I sell the diner, it could give me the capital I need."

"How? Any money you make from the sale will have to go to purchasing a new one, unless you're thinking of renting. You own the diner free and clear, don't you?"

"Yes," she admitted.

"There you go. You may be operating on a shoestring budget now, but it'll perk up."

Sophie put her hands up in the air. "How am I supposed to say no when both of you are wearing me down?"

"Good." Ginny grinned happily.

Jody stood up. "Come on. I'll follow you to your apartment and call Knox to tell him you're on your way. You can pick out what you want to move to the trailer, and I'll bring it back so you'll have it waiting for you when you get off work."

"You don't need to go with me. I can load what I want to take in my car—"

"It'll be quicker if I go with you. That way, you can go on to the diner. Ginny can open it for you."

"Are you sure?" she asked Ginny.

"I'd love to. My sister-in-law is babysitting for me. She'll be upset if I told her I didn't need her."

"If you're sure ..." She looked at both of them.

"We are." Jody reached for their coffee cups.

Handing Ginny the keys to the restaurant, Sophie allowed Jody to usher her out of the house.

She took in the beauty of the surroundings and couldn't believe she was going to be able to live here. Owning a restaurant wasn't her only dream; she had dreamed of having enough money to live in a wide-open space with trees and grass, where she had her own yard, even a puppy. She really, really wanted a puppy.

"Are you ready?" Jody brought her back from her imaginings.

"Sorry. It's beautiful here. Ginny's lucky."

"We all are. We each have a section of property on the mountain. We own over seventy acres. If you close the diner before dark, I can show you the trailer while it's still light enough to see."

"Okay."

Walking to her car, she was conscious of Jody following behind her.

"I'll meet you at your apartment. My truck is parked at Silas' house." Jody pointed to the small road branching off

Ginny's driveway. "Take that road. When you come to the end, make a right. That will lead you straight into town."

"I remember driving here last night."

"Cool. I'll see you there."

Relieved when Jody left, she got into her car, happy she could drop the poker face she had to maintain anytime he was near her; it was becoming harder to do. When she was near his vicinity, she felt as if there was an electrical charge coming off him. The closer she was to him, the stronger the charge she felt. Just thinking about it made her feel silly.

Following Jody's directions, she drove into town without incident. The sheriff was already there with his squad car parked out front.

"Sophie."

Shaking the hand he held out to her, she made a face at the apartment building. "I dread going inside," she confessed.

"Don't be. Baylin is in a holding cell until after you come to a decision."

"I'm sorry I didn't call you back. It's been overwhelming to find out a neighbor could do this to me. At least you were able to get her to confess."

"I had nothing to do with her confession. Jody figured it out and had a talk with her. Baylin probably confessed because it was safer to than getting on the bad side of the Coleman clan."

Shocked at what the sheriff had said, it took a minute for her to respond. "Why would she be afraid of the Colemans? They've been very sweet to me."

The way the sheriff stared at her, she didn't think the Colemans and sweet had been used in the same sentence before.

"They aren't nice?"

"Sweet? Nice? I wouldn't use those terms to describe

them. They stay to themselves, stay out of town, and don't make trouble unless you go looking for it."

"And if someone does?"

"Then I would advise them not to. There are two clans in this town who will shoot you dead if you hurt something that belongs to them. The Colemans is one."

"Who's the other?"

"The Porters."

"Doesn't Greer Porter work for you?"

The sheriff's face twisted into a painful grimace. "Don't remind me."

"I've met him." Sophie laughed. "I can't say I blame you."

"You ready to go inside?"

Sophie looked around. Jody wasn't there yet. "Jody was supposed to meet me here."

The sheriff nodded. "When I talked to him, he said he needed to drop some groceries off at the diner for Ginny and would come right over when he was finished."

"All right, I guess we can go inside."

Her breathing escalated as they started through the door.

"There's Jody, parking."

Looking to where the sheriff was pointing, she felt her breathing slow down. She put on her poker face as they waited for Jody and lowered her eyes when he came to stand with them at the elevator.

All three of them filed into the elevator when it opened. Jody and the sheriff discussed the weather as they rode upward. Then the sheriff walked ahead of them as they stepped off the elevator.

"Thank you for dropping the groceries off at the diner. I'm glad Ginny remembered they were in the refrigerator."

"No problem." Jody gave her a questioning glance as they neared her door. "Are you up for this?"

"I guess I have to be, don't I?"

Jody pulled her to a stop. "No, you don't. I can pack everything up that isn't broken and take pictures of what is. The boys and I can clean up and have it ready for when your parents arrive."

"I can't ask you to do that for me."

"You aren't asking. I'm offering."

"I can do this." Sophie strengthened her resolve. "Besides, I have to get out of these jeans—they're cutting me in two."

Chapter Eighteen

Sophie stared at the vindictive rage that had taken place in her bedroom. Walking over a broken vase with fake flowers, she picked up the stuffed toy poodle that had been torn apart. She clutched the ragged remains in her arms and sank down onto the bed.

"Are you all right?" she heard Jody ask through the buzzing in her head.

"Sophie?"

"She killed Pixie." She felt the tears sliding out of the corner of her eyes but couldn't make her hands move away from Pixie. "It's the only toy Marty ever gave me."

"I'm sorry, baby."

Numbly, she was aware of Jody sitting down on the bed next to her and pulling her into his arms.

"She could have destroyed anything, and I could have taken it, but not Pixie." Crying into his shoulder, she couldn't make herself stop no matter how hard she tried. "Marty wouldn't let me have a dog. Mom said I wouldn't shut up about wanting one. And she wouldn't get me one because she was afraid he would hurt it when we had to leave them alone together. I know he only gave it to me to shut me up. Pixie was the only nice thing he ever did for me. When I was lonely or depressed, Pixie was always there for me, and I didn't have to take him out." She cried harder.

"I would get you another one, but I know it won't make up for it." Jody ran his hand through her hair, tilting her head back. "Pixie isn't the only thing he's ever given you," he reminded her. "He left the diner to you."

"You see how well that's working out, don't you?"

He lifted her to her feet. "You're going to stop crying, and let's find you something to change into. You'll feel better when you're not being sawed in two by Ginny's jeans."

Sophie opened the dresser drawer containing her pants. The smell coming from inside had her stepping back. "Why do they smell that way?"

Jody hadn't moved away, pulling the drawer out further. "She smashed rotten eggs on them."

She started gagging, and Jody hastily closed the drawer before going through the rest of her drawers. "Baylin went through all the drawers. Do you keep your clothes anywhere else?"

"I had a laundry basket with dirty clothes in the bathroom."

"Stay here, and I'll get them."

Sophie didn't argue.

Jody wasn't gone long before he came back out, shutting the door behind him. "She got those, too."

"How many rotten eggs did that woman have?"

"She didn't use eggs on those."

Sophie closed her eyes, not wanting to ask what she had used.

"Sophie."

The sheriff calling her name from the doorway had her lifting her lids to stare at him.

"Seeing this, do you want to change your mind about pressing charges?"

"I don't know. I never imagined it to be this bad. How do I know she won't do the same thing when my parents move in here?"

"She won't," the sheriff assured her. "If so much as a leaf blows in here, I'll lock her up. If she comes within fifty feet of you, I'll lock her up. She's also going to pay you for the damage she's done to your property."

"None of my things cost very much. I mainly bought from thrift stores."

"You'll be reimbursed." The sheriff glanced around. "Anything salvageable?"

"No."

"Then let's go. Jacob and I can take care of this while you're working," Jody told her.

"No. I'll come in the morning and bring some trash bags."

"There's another option," Jody suggested. "If you don't want Jacob and me taking care of it for you, hire a cleaning company, and Baylin can pay for it."

That suggestion, she could go for.

"I'll do that."

They locked up the apartment and went down the elevator. It was only when they reached the door that Sophie thought to ask a question.

"How did she get inside? I know I locked the door."

"The maintenance man let her in," the sheriff answered. "I'm going to make sure Alan gets his share of community service, too. Baylin told him that you called and asked her to check to make sure you had turned the stove off."

"Alan and Baylin used to date. I'm sure it didn't take much for her to convince him to open the door."

"Has she ever acted this way over other men she's dated?"

"As far as I know, I'm the only one who's had to deal with this psychotic side of her."

The sheriff told them that he would be in touch when Baylin paid for the damages, leaving when he got a call over his radio.

Jody looked at her worriedly. "Do you feel up to going to the diner?"

"Yes, I need to keep my mind occupied. Thank you for coming with me. I didn't expect for it to be that bad."

"Glad to help." He walked with her to her car.

She pressed the unlock button and got inside.

"I'll see you at the restaurant."

"You don't have to come. I can handle it until Logan comes in. I don't expect any more customers than I had yesterday," she said glumly, starting the car.

"You should be more positive," he chastised her.

"Okay ... I'm positive today is going to suck as badly as yesterday."

Chapter Nineteen

When Sophie opened the diner door, she came to a full stop. Was she imagining that she had not one but eleven customers?

"Looks like business is picking up," Jody commented by her side.

Ginny was taking an order at one table while Logan was behind the counter, making drinks.

Upon seeing her, Ginny excused herself from the customers. "You had four waiting at the door when I opened." She nodded her head at the customers whose orders she had just taken. "They ordered pancakes and sausages. Tell Logan to get them coffee then come out back, and I'll teach you how to make pancakes."

Blinking tears back, she reached out to hug Ginny. "I don't know how to thank you."

"Keep that in mind when you have to start milking the goats."

They broke apart and went into the kitchen, where Ginny showed her how to make the pancake batter while the sausages were frying.

"Pour it into a squirt bottle," she instructed. Then, once the batter was in the squirt bottle, she squirted a circle on the grill. "When you see it bubbling in the middle, place a finger on the pancake, and if you can see you fingerprint, flip it. When the edges are brown, it's done. *Voila!* You made pancakes."

Sophie made several more before she got used to gauging when to flip and when they were done.

The rest of the morning went by fast as Logan and Jody worked at the front of the restaurant while Ginny and her made the food. At one point, Sophie peeked through the door and saw the restaurant was half-filled.

"Feeling more positive about the restaurant?" Ginny asked as she slid two pans of meatloaf in the oven.

"Yes. I don't know what turned it around, but at least I can see a light at the end of the tunnel."

"I'm glad. I'd hate to lose my new friend. Besides, I need someone to make meatloaf for—my brothers are sick of it."

Laughing, they got back to work.

"New ticket."

Sophie looked up from making a plate to see Logan's face as he placed the ticket in the window. She thought something was wrong, so she stood on her tippy toes to look through the window. "Something going on?"

Ginny came to look out, too.

Jody was checking a customer out while Logan was carrying a tray of drinks to a group of teenagers sitting at a back table.

"Are they friends of Logan's?"

Was that why Logan had looked unhappy when he clipped the ticket in the window? Sophie could understand it might be embarrassing for him to wait on his friends, especially when there were several girls at the table.

"I wish." Ginny sighed. "The boy sitting next to the

blonde girl and the girl with the pink sweater is Fynn. He's my younger brother. Logan and Fynn don't get along."

Logan was a sweet young man, so she couldn't understand anyone disliking him.

"Do you know why?"

Ginny shook her head. "We've been letting them work it out on their own. Silas and Logan's uncle Greer used to hate each other, but they get along now."

"I see."

When Logan turned around after leaving the drinks, she could hear mocking laughter following him.

Sophie saw red.

Dropping from her tippy toes, she strode out of the kitchen, prepared to let Fynn have a piece of her mind. She cleared the door, her intention on asking Fynn to leave, only to have Jody beat her to the table. Before Fynn could react, Jody pulled him up by the back of his shirt and dragged him to the front of the restaurant.

"Quit it, Jody," Fynn hissed at his brother.

Jody barked at Logan, "Give me the apron."

Startled, Logan untied the apron at his waist and handed it to him.

Jody took the apron and threw it at Fynn.

"Put it on," Jody snapped. "You're working for the rest of the day."

"I'm not."

"Yes, you are, and when you're done, you can explain to Silas why you were late for dinner." Jody turned to look at Logan. "Logan, you're done for the day. Fynn will work the rest of your shift, and you won't lose any money. Sophie will give you Fynn's pay."

Fynn shot daggers at Jody. "That's not fair."

"I don't think it's fair the way you embarrassed Logan, so you can take his place while *you* wait on *him*."

"No." Fynn's voice dropped so low that Sophie could barely hear the exchange between the brothers.

"No?"

Sophie looked around at Ginny.

"Stay out of it," Ginny warned her. "Let Jody deal with this. Come on; we left the grill unattended."

She hesitated but was relieved when Fynn reluctantly tied the apron around his waist. As she went back into the kitchen, she protectively looked to watch Logan grab his jacket and leave.

Ginny sighed when she saw Logan leave, also. "I'll be glad when they grow out of this stage."

"How long did it take for Silas and Greer?"

Ginny picked up the ticket that Logan had put down. "I think their late twenties." Ginny saw the concern on her face. "Don't worry; Fynn is going through a stage. I don't think it will take him and Logan that long to become friends."

Sophie wasn't so sure.

"The problem is both of them have had a crush on the same girl since they were little kids."

"Ouch."

"Yes. Eventually, they'll work it out. She'll chose one of them, or one of the boys will fall for another girl."

"So, all that was over a girl?"

Ginny turned away to drop fries in the fry basket. "Both of the boys are very gifted. There may be a power struggle going on between them as well. Luckily, Silas and Dustin, Logan's father, are aware of the situation and try to keep the boys apart."

"Until something like today happens," Sophie finished for her.

"Yes. When that happens, Jody and Greer step in."

"What do they do?"

"Greer takes Logan fishing."

"What does Jody do?"

Ginny's lips turned into a mischievous smile. "Brings him back down to earth."

Chapter Twenty

Sophie carried the bags of clothes she had bought at the thrift store across the street from the diner. Ginny had suggested the store when she explained the purple sweatpants Jody had dropped off for her from Walmart before going to the diner to get her out of Ginny's jeans.

Ginny grinned when she saw her walk back into the diner. "I see you had a successful shopping trip."

"That's one of the best thrift stores I have ever been inside of." Sophie told her, stuffing the bags under the counter except for one, which she placed on the counter. "I met a woman named Lily. She was so stinking beautiful I would hate her if she weren't so nice."

Ginny laughed. "I know. It sucks when they're nice."

"Girl, I'm allowed to complain; you're not." Sophie rolled her eyes. "You don't look as if a train ran over you then backed up to hit you again."

Ginny shook her head. "You're very pretty."

"Maybe in another universe," Sophie scoffed, fiddling with her messy bun. "I need to get my hair done. These glasses need to go, too. Thanks to Baylin, I'm out of contacts. My prescription is out, and to get it redone, I need to go to the eye doctor."

"You have had your challenges since coming here," Ginny commiserated. "By the way, Jody needed to take off when the customers died down. I have Fynn in the back, mopping the floor.

"He doesn't need to do that."

"Yes, he does," she said firmly. "The more jobs he does here, the easier it will be for Silas. He hates to punish Fynn; he prefers being the big brother than having to be the disciplinarian."

"I wish I had a brother like Silas."

"I'm very blessed." Ginny eyed the items Sophie was pulling out of the bag. "I see Lily told you about the bakery Willa runs upstairs of the thrift store.

Sophie took out the raspberry cheesecake, an apple pie, and chocolate cupcakes.

"Help yourself."

Ginny didn't have to be told twice. Pouring herself a glass of milk, she nabbed a chocolate cupcake and sat down at the kitchen counter.

The tingling of the bell had both their heads turning to see Deputy Bevere walk inside. He took a seat at the counter and eyed the variety of desserts.

"Hello, Deputy, what can I get you?" Sophie greeted him.

"I'll have one of those of cupcakes, a cup of coffee to go, and you can call me Joel."

Sophie felt a heated flush fill her checks as his eyes met hers.

She filled his order, then felt self-conscious when she turned around and caught him still watching her.

"I was wondering if you're doing anything Saturday night? There's a music festival going on at the park. Everyone takes blankets and coolers to watch the performances."

"Sounds like fun, but I'm afraid I won't be able to. I don't close the diner until ten."

"You'll be wasting your time. Everyone will be at the festival. There will also be food and drink booths."

Sophie bit her lip then nodded. *Why not?*

"Okay. I'd like to go," she agreed, sliding his order across the counter.

Joel stood, picked his order up, and went to the cash register.

"I'll pick you up at six." He gave her his card then looked toward Ginny. "Are you going to be singing Saturday?"

"I'm supposed to go on at seven, but I expect it to be more at eight."

"I'll see you ladies Saturday. Do you want me to pick you up here, Sophie, or your apartment?"

"You can pick me up here," she replied, giving him his card back.

Sophie glanced at Ginny as she finished drinking her milk while Joel left. "I didn't know you sang."

"I'm a woman of many talents."

"I see that." Finding a display case under the counter, she filled it with the desserts.

Ginny rose and picked up the empty glass. "Do you like Joel?"

"What's not to like? He's very attractive and seems nice."

"He is."

Sophie raised an eyebrow at her gloomy tone. "What's wrong?"

"Nothing. I was just hoping you ... I thought you and Jody were hitting it off."

"You thought I liked ... *like* Jody?"

"You don't?"

"I know he's your brother, but I would never look at Jody romantically."

Ginny's mouth dropped. "Why not? Is it because of Baylin?"

Sophie leaned her hip against the counter. "No ... Maybe a little. But I stay away from men like Jody."

"What's wrong with Jody?" Sisterly outrage poured out of Ginny.

"Nothing. He's been really good to me, helping out here, and I honestly don't think I would have made it through this morning without him."

"Then what's—"

"Ginny, you may be his sister, but have you noticed how women react around him?"

Ginny's outrage vanished and was replaced with a pained expression. "It's hard to miss," she acknowledged.

"They can't keep their hands off him, and he must be a breast man, because they love flashing their boobs at him. They aren't even discreet about it. The woman who falls in love with Jody is going to have to have thick skin, be willing to overlook his wandering past, and deal with trust issues each time when they're apart. I'm not that woman.

"Look at me, Ginny. I'm a four on a one-to-ten scale, and I'm being generous to myself. Jody is a twenty just wearing jeans and a T-shirt. I don't want to know what he would look like all dressed up."

"Joel isn't exactly chopped liver," Ginny argued.

"No. He's a ten, a normal ten." Sophie put both her hands up, mimicking a scale. "This is Joel." Sophie put one of her hands out in front of her. "This is Jody." Her other hand went way higher than Joel's. "With Joel, at least I stand a chance of keeping him faithful. Jody ... not a chance in hell."

"Jody could be faithful to his soul mate."

"Good for her. She's a better person than me."

Ginny gave her a mysterious smile. "You never know ... She could be *just* like you."

Chapter Twenty-One

The trailer looked cozy and comfortable. Sophie stared around the living room that had two sofas before wandering over to the small kitchen. "It's cute."

Jody winced at her description.

"Are you sure I'm not inconveniencing your family?"

"Not at all," he lied, taking a seat on one of the sofas.

"None of you live in here?"

"I stay over at Jacob's most of the time."

Sophie turned to stare at him. "This is *your* home?"

"When I'm here, which isn't often," he explained. "Jacob gets a better Wi-Fi signal than I do. We like to play computer games at night. His speed is better than mine."

"My dad likes to play games, too."

"Your stepdad?"

"My dad," she corrected him. "I don't think of Marty as being my father."

"I'm sorry."

Sophie shrugged. "Don't be. Some parents are shitty. My mom and dad made up for Marty. They protected me from him. We had to move from state to state. No matter how hard they tried, Marty would find us, and he would make our lives a living hell. He would find my parents, call them, and make terrible threats to them. To tell you the truth, I felt relief when the lawyer contacted me to tell me he was dead. I would have thanked whoever killed him, but now it seems he may be the one who wants that money Marty owes him."

"Don't worry about him. The sheriff and Greer are keeping their eyes out for him, and he can't get on our land without us knowing he's here."

"I'm glad you have cameras here. It makes me feel safer."

"Good. I want you to feel safe." Jody rose from the couch, neglecting to tell her there wasn't a camera on the property. "The fridge is full. Feel free to eat anything you want."

Jody noticed, when he stood up, she moved farther into the kitchen, putting the counter between them. Whenever he drew close to her, she always managed to place herself away from him. The only time she allowed him in her private space was when she was tired or upset.

"Ginny said you're going out with Joel to the music festival."

"Yes, he seems like a nice man."

"He is," Jody agreed. "He's good people."

"That's good to know."

"He's just not for you."

Her eyes widened at his words. "Why not?"

"You're wasting his time, and yours, too."

"I don't know why you think that. You've only known me for a few days."

"You'd be surprised at what I know. For instance, I'm aware you're attracted to me."

"I'm not."

Jody clicked his tongue at her. "Don't lie. I wasn't the only one who felt as if lightning struck when we first saw each other."

Her cheeks flushed a bright red. "You're a very attractive man, but that doesn't mean I'm attracted to you."

He clicked his tongue at her again. "Another lie? There's no need to be embarrassed. I'm very attracted to you, too."

Stiffly, she came from behind the counter to snatch up the bags she had brought into the trailer. "I should have known this was too good to be true."

Jody blocked her path to the door. "There's no need to get on your high horse. I don't expect you to sleep with me just because we're giving you a place to stay. All I'm doing is putting it out there that I'm interested in you. I'm not getting regulated to the friend zone just because you're afraid to admit you're attracted to me." Jody turned toward the door to let himself out. "See you tomorrow. Sleep well."

He closed the door behind him. After what he had said, he would be lucky to find himself in the friend zone with her.

As he strode to Silas' house, he wanted to take his frustration out on Deputy Bevere for daring to ask Sophie out. She was going out with Joel, who had nailed more women than he had ever considered doing.

He walked up the steps and went through the front door without knocking. Silas and Fynn were sitting in the living room. Fynn was staring at Silas defiantly as Silas broke off from talking to him.

"What's going on?" Jody asked, throwing himself down onto the couch next to Silas.

"What do you care? You're just like Silas—both of you just take up for Logan."

"Why wouldn't we?" Jody stretched his legs out to prop his feet on the living room table. "Logan doesn't do anything to you, yet you're constantly picking on him."

Fynn's expression lost steam. "I don't know why. There's something about him that sets me on edge."

Silas regarded Fynn seriously. "I've told you why. Your gifts are combating with Logan's. You have to get better control of yours."

"So, Logan is stronger than me?" Fynn snorted. "Not likely."

Jody removed his legs from the table. "He damn sure has better control of his. I'm older than you, and all of us have gifts. Greer won't acknowledge any of his family have gifts, but we know they do. We can feel the power coming from them. Don't underestimate them. We've managed to keep the peace between that side of our family tree by controlling our gifts. The Porters and the Colemans have to work together to keep our secrets safe. Silas and Greer, as much as they disliked each other, put their differences aside for the best interest of our families."

Fynn made a face. "You want me to be friends with Logan?"

Jody turned as serious as Silas. "Some of your gifts are earth-based, like mine. Logan has to have at least one earth-based one, too. Like magnets when in various directions, they can repel each other. I feel his energy when I'm near Logan. I'm older and more experienced, so I can counter the energy by moving my position when I'm around him. You have to learn how to react to your gift, not let it control you."

At his explanation, Fynn seemed to be thinking over what he had said. "I didn't think about it that way."

"We're all willing to help you, Fynn. We all love you. To be honest, I don't know how well I would have managed having as many gifts piled on me like you do. I have trouble managing mine. I do keep one thing in my mind always, though—when I make a mistake, not only could I pay the price, but someone else in our family might. Our gifts come with a price. We lost Leah much too young because of her gifts. We don't want to lose you, too."

Fynn nodded. "May I go upstairs now?"

"Yes," Silas allowed him.

Jody and Silas stared at each other as Fynn went up the steps. Jody spoke only once he heard Fynn's door closing.

"You think he will listen to us?"

Silas' lips twisted into a half-smile. "Did you listen to my warnings?"

Jody chuckled. "No. But, to be fair, I've given you the least amount of trouble compared to the rest of us."

Silas made a scoffing sound. "So far. I heard Joel asked Sophie out. Are you going to behave?"

Jody gave him an innocent look. "Absolutely."

Chapter Twenty-Two

Spotting the man he was looking for, Jody pulled his truck up next to Joel's, then pressed a button to roll his window down and motioned for the deputy to do the same.

Joel rested his arm on the window edge once it was down. "What's up, Jody?"

"Nothing much," he answered cordially. "What are you up to? Casing the park?"

"Nope, just hiding out from Greer until I get off shift. I can't be near him with a loaded gun."

"He does tend to get on people's nerves," Jody agreed.

"What are you doing out so early?"

"Wanted to have a chat with you."

Joel frowned. "About what?"

Jody dropped his cordial attitude. "I heard you asked Sophie to the music festival."

"I did." Joel gave him a knowing smirk. "What's wrong? I beat you to the punch?"

"She's not exactly your type, is she?"

"She's not exactly yours, either."

"She's exactly my type. I want you to cancel the date."

"Why in the fuck should I do that?"

"Because I'm asking you to."

"Yeah. Sorry, but not sorry. I'm looking forward to it."

"Then I guess I'll be keeping my date with Sherree."

The laughter died on Joel's face. "Stay away from my sister," he warned.

"I will if you stay away from Sophie. I give something up, you give something up. Sounds fair to me."

"You don't want to make an enemy out of me, Jody Coleman. Anytime I catch you in town, I'll arrest your ass."

Jody gave him a careless shrug. "That'll only make Sherree like me more. Hell, I might be your brother-in-law by the end of summer."

Joel lowered his eyelids to half-mast. "I'll kill you first."

"You, a police officer, threating me?" Jody raised his voice as if he was surprised.

"Son of a bitch, you win. I'll cancel. But If I catch you sniffing around my sister, I'll put a bullet in you dick."

"See, I knew we could come to an agreement. You have a nice day."

"Fuck off."

"Same."

Jody rolled his window back up and drove out of the park as he whistled along to a tune on the radio. That encounter had gone much easier than he had expected. Thankfully, he didn't have to resort to harsher tactics. Sophie might have thought her date was a done deal, but the only way he would let another man near her was over his cold, dead body. He made a turn onto a side street, then cut his wheels to turn into a parking lot.

Getting out of his truck, he walked sedately into an apartment building that he was getting fucking sick of coming to.

He pressed the elevator button and went inside when it

opened, got off on the floor he needed, and walked down the quiet hallway. After tapping on the door, he waited patiently for it to open.

"What are you doing here?" Sophie asked, opening the door wider for him to come inside.

Jody went inside and took the apartment in. "I see you decided not to hire a cleaning company."

Red filled her cheeks. "I didn't want anyone to have to deal with this mess."

"Okay." Jody rolled the sleeves of his long-sleeved Henley up. "Where are the trash bags?"

Sophie gave what sounded like a frustrated sigh. "Thank you, but I've got this."

"Me leaving is not an option," he stated firmly. "If we work together, we can get two rooms tackled before you have to open the restaurant."

When she stomped off into the kitchen to get a box of trash bags, he felt safe enough to mutter. "Have you seen anything like this before?"

"Who are you talking to?" she asked, looking a bit concerned when she came back.

"Uh, no one. Just myself," he clarified before clearing his throat and changing the subject. "So, do you want me to work in here with you, or should I tackle another room?"

Seeing the indecision on her face, Jody offered a suggestion. "I can do the bathroom."

"No! I'll do the bathroom."

"Sophie, there isn't anything in there that will shock me or gross me out. I've already seen it. Is there anything in there you want to keep?"

"No," she mumbled.

"Then at least let me take that off your chest."

"I can't ask you to clean—"

"You didn't ask; I offered. I feel bad Baylin took her anger out on you. This will make me feel better."

"Go ahead."

"Atta girl." Giving her a jaunty smile, he went into the bedroom to go into the bathroom, then opened the trash bag and got to work. He had a strong stomach, but what Baylin had done to the bathroom was disgusting.

He had known Sophie wouldn't want strangers going through her things. Nor would she want Ginny to see it, either. Sophie wasn't used to letting people help her, other than her parents. He imagined moving from state to state as she said they had. They had learned to depend on each other, Jody thought grimly. The woman was just going to have to get used to the fact her inner circle was going to expand. She had a big family who would take her family's back to ease their worries.

He made a mental note of the makeup that Baylin had destroyed before he tossed it in the trash bag. Using the few washcloths that had managed to escape her notice, he cleaned the bathroom. Luckily, he found some bleach under the sink.

Satisfied, he tied up the trash bag. All he needed to do now was sweep the floor and mop.

When he went back to living room, he found Sophie had made headway, also.

"Where's your broom and mop?"

"In the hall closet."

Hearing a tearful note in her voice, he sent her a questioning glance. "Is something wrong?"

Sophie gave him a worried frown. "I'm wondering how I'm going to be able to replace the couch, chair, and glass table. The cost is more than I made for the whole week so far. I'll have to pay for it before my parents move in. I already told them I managed to scrape enough together to furnish the apartment."

"Put that out of your mind. Baylin will take care of the cost of the furniture. By the time your parents get here, it will look just as it did before she trashed your belongings."

"You think?"

"I do," he said firmly. "I'm going to finish up in the bathroom; you finish what you need to get done here. When we're done, I'll help you open the restaurant. I'll even make you my famous cinnamon rolls."

The worry disappeared from her face and was replaced with humor. "What makes them famous?"

"No one in town can beat them. I've won two blue ribbons at the fair for those suckers."

Sophie laughed. "Then I can't wait to taste them."

Warmth filled his chest at the way she looked at him. Then regret filled him that he hadn't been true to her the way Matthew had stayed to Alanna.

He found the mop and broom and finished the bathroom.

"You ready?" he asked, laying the trash bag on the floor.

"As much as I can do for now. I'll do the rest tonight after I close the diner."

Jody carried out the trash bags and pressed the elevator button while Sophie closed and locked the apartment door.

As he waited for her, she was turning away from the door when Baylin came out of her apartment, dressed for work. He groaned inwardly.

Both women stood indecisively as to what to do next. Sophie made the first move by starting to walk down the hallway. Baylin opened her door and went back inside her apartment.

Seeing Baylin had gone back inside, Jody could read the relief on Sophie's expression.

"Well, that was uncomfortable," she remarked, stepping inside the waiting elevator.

"The only one who should have been uncomfortable was Baylin."

As the elevator door closed, he pressed the first-floor button.

"Do you think, if she gets another man, she could do the same thing? That's scary what she did. I don't think I want my parents living next door to her."

Jody thought it over. "I'm hoping she's learned her lesson, but I can understand why you don't want your parents to live next to her."

"What should I do?"

"You won't have to do a damn thing," he said with certainly. "Baylin is going to have to move."

Chapter Twenty-Three

S ophie was heartened by the couple of customers waiting in their cars and the six waiting by the door as Jody and she arrived at the restaurant.

As she set her purse under the counter, she received a text.

Jody, who was already behind the counter, looked at her quizzically as she read the message.

"Ginny said she won't be able to work today. Freddie woke up with a sick stomach, and she doesn't think it's wise to come here until she makes sure it isn't contagious," she said, reading the text off to him.

"Smart move. I'm not anxious to share that with my nephew."

"Me neither." Setting her phone down, she reached for her apron in preparation to go to the kitchen.

"Why don't you let me handle the food today, and you wait the tables? That way, I can make the cinnamon rolls."

"You know how to cook?"

"Silas made sure we can cook to pitch in when needed. Go take care of the customers. I promise I won't poison anyone."

She made a face at him but didn't argue. She hated cooking, and he couldn't do worse than George, nor her. Ginny had been doing the majority of the cooking, so she was more than happy to turn it over to him.

The morning ran smoothly with Jody working the grill, making breakfast. After serving a large table, she went back to the kitchen to Jody saying something. "What's that?" she asked, thinking he heard her come in.

"Oh, nothing." He shrugged her off. "Did you need something?"

"No, I'm just very impressed," she complimented him. "Will you be able to do lunch, too?"

"Hamburgers are my third specialty," he boasted. "Were you able to taste the cinnamon rolls?"

"They sold out before I could."

Jody pulled a plate out of the microwave. "I had an idea you would. I saved you one."

He watched as Sophie picked up the cinnamon roll. Grinning when her eyes nearly rolled back, he felt his body surge with lust when she licked a dollop of frosting from the corner of her mouth.

"Jody, these are fantastic!"

He leaned forward, intent on kissing her, when the sound of the bell ringing over the door had him groaning.

"I know, right?" She scrunched up her nose. "That bell is getting on my nerves, too."

Jody peeked through the kitchen window to see who had come into the restaurant. His jaw clenched. It was Joel, who gave her a flirtatious smile as he sat at the front counter.

"I'm all out of cupcakes." Jody heard her apologize to him.

"That's okay. I'll just take a cup of coffee to go."

"You just missed getting one of Jody's cinnamon rolls," Sophie told him as she poured his coffee.

"I did? Jody made cinnamon rolls for you to sell?"

Jody met Joel's eyes as he talked to Sophie.

"Yes, he did," Sophie enthused.

"Damn. I'm sorry I missed tasting one. He usually makes it for women he's ..." Jody seemed to be thinking of a polite way to describe the relationship he shared with the women he made the rolls for. "Seeing."

"Oh."

Jody could tell she was at a loss for words. Fortunately, he didn't have the same problem. Swinging the kitchen door open, he moved toward the counter.

"Hey, Joel. Good to see you."

"Jody. How are you doing?"

"Doing good. What can we get you?"

"Sophie's taking care of me. I don't have time to eat. I'm driving my sister to Louisville. My grandmother isn't feeling well, so Sherree will be staying with her until she feels better."

"I'm sorry to hear that. I hope she feels better soon."

Jody had to restrain himself from leaping over the counter at the triumphant look he gave him. He had made his move, and Joel had countered him.

"Thanks. How much do I owe you, Sophie?"

"The coffee is on the house, Joel."

"Thanks, I appreciate it. Jody, see you around."

Jody nodded, letting Joel almost reach the door.

"Oh ... Joel. Game on."

Joel lifted two fingers to his forehead and gave him a sarcastic salute.

When he turned around, he saw Sophie staring at him curiously.

"What did that mean?"

"Joel plays games with Jacob and me. I was just reminding him that we have a game coming up."

"I don't know how guys get so into games."

"Some more than others."

He went back into the kitchen to start filling the orders

for the large tables. After lunch, Jody saw the restaurant had emptied out. After washing his hands, he went to the front of the restaurant, where Sophie and Logan were cleaning tables.

"Sophie, where do you keep the light bulbs?"

"I'll show you."

Taking the dishes to the busing station, she went to the kitchen and showed him.

Reaching for them on the top shelf of the metal unit that held the restaurant supplies, he grabbed one of the bulbs then looked around the kitchen. "Where's the step ladder?"

Sophie looked up at the ceiling where the bulb was out then went back to the metal unit.

"It was here yesterday, behind the paper cup box."

Jody moved the box so they could clearly look behind it. "Could Ginny or Fynn have moved it?"

"Possibly, but I don't see where."

Sophie texted Fynn, Ginny, and asked Logan. None of them were aware of where it was.

"I suppose I could climb up on a chair," she said.

"You won't be tall enough to reach, and I don't trust my weight on one of those chairs upfront—they are older than I am," Jody joked. "Here, I have an idea."

Handing her the light bulb, Jody placed his hands on her hips and lifted her toward the ceiling.

"What are you doing?" she sputtered.

"Letting you change the light bulb. Can you reach it?"

"Uh ... yes, give me a second."

Jody held her steady as she twisted out the burned-out bulb and screwed in the new one.

"Got it." Her hand went to his shoulder.

Jody pulled her closer to him as he slowly slid her down until her eyes were level with his. "Good job."

"Thank you."

"You're welcome." He set her back down onto her feet. "Anytime. Glad to be of help."

Jody narrowed his eyes on Sophie as she fled out of the kitchen, nearly colliding with Logan.

He placed the tub of dishes in the sink as Logan eyed him. "I could have sworn that ladder was there yesterday when I needed to refill the drink station."

"Yeah." Jody shrugged, beginning to load the dishwasher. "It's probably misplaced. I'm sure it'll show up."

"I'm sure it will."

Jody's lips twitched at Logan's ironic tone. "You going to tell on me?"

Logan looked at him speculatively. "No, I'm just surprised you didn't use the opportunity to kiss her. That was what I thought you were going to do."

"Ah ... You should watch the original *Star Wars*." Jody shook his head. "You have to time your first shot just right to get the explosion you want. That was a trial run. Watch and learn ... young jedi."

Chapter Twenty-Four

"You mind making a couple of those sandwiches for me?" Jody asked.

Sophie looked up from the prep table. "Not at all. What do you want on them?"

"Everything but onions, and the pickled peppers."

Blushing at the wink Jody gave her, she went back to wrapping the sandwiches she had made for Joel and her.

"How many would you like?"

"Just two."

"You don't want to check with your date what she would like on her sandwich?"

"No need. Both sandwiches are for me. I'm going with the family. Ginny and Alanna are both packing coolers, but I want to take extra for me. My brothers won't hesitate to eat mine if I'm late."

Sophie didn't ask herself why she was much happier making the sandwiches for Jody after hearing he wasn't taking a date.

"What time is Joel picking you up?"

"At six." Sophie finished wrapping Jody's sandwiches. "Want me to put them in the fridge?"

"Yes, please. I left my cooler in my truck. I'll take the sandwiches when I leave."

Logan poked his head through the door. "You mind if I leave, Sophie? My dad is here to pick me up."

"Of course. Have fun tonight." Sophie smiled as Logan left.

She really liked Logan. He was a sweet kid. He was very introverted, so she sympathized with him, as she had been an introvert at his age, also. It had taken her years to come out of her shell. If not for a friend of hers, she didn't think she would have.

"I want to get changed. Would you mind watching the restaurant while I do that?"

Jody handed her a hamburger plate. "Go ahead. I'm all caught up until someone comes in. When you get done, I need to get changed, too."

"Deal."

In the bathroom, she changed into a new pair of jeans that she had splurged on in a regular department store. Carefully removing a sweater from her duffle bag, she pulled it on. She had recognized the designer label when she saw it in the thrift store. It was rose-colored, and she had fallen in love with it when she had seen it on one of the tables. She hated to put her sensible shoes back on, but she still had another half an hour before she could close the restaurant. Applying the minimum of makeup, which Ginny had generously supplied, she lightly put on a foundation then brushed on some blush. When she was satisfied, she rolled on some mascara before putting her glasses back on.

"I guess this is the best you're going to get."

She zipped her duffle bag and left the restroom to find Jody mumbling to himself again, wondering if she should start to be concerned about the amounts of times she found him speaking to no one. She decided to let it go figuring it must be a strange habit Jody had. Hell, she was known to talk to herself from time to time as well.

"Your turn." While sliding the bag under the counter, she was aware of Jody's assessing gaze as he slid his own bag out from under the counter.

Sophie rolled silverware, waiting for the minutes to click by. She was putting the utensils away when Jody came out of the restroom.

Struck speechless, she was terrified she had swallowed her tongue when he bent next to her to put his bag away. Then the faint hint of his cologne only heightened her awareness of him.

Moving away from him, she started closing the register to give herself breathing room. If she stayed close to him, she wouldn't be able to keep from rubbing against him, begging to be stroked.

She couldn't blame women who came to the restaurant, constantly seeking his attention.

"I guess I'll take off, unless you need me to do something for you?"

She did, but nothing she would let him do unless she wanted to end up a basket case like Baylin.

"No, I'm good. Have fun tonight."

"You, too."

Thankfully, she was able to hold on to her restraint until Jody left.

When he had walked out of the restroom dressed in nice jeans lovingly hugging his body, her reaction had almost slipped under her guard. The black sweater molded to his upper body, except around the neck, where the turtleneck was bunched like a thick gray scarf. He slayed.

It just wasn't fair that Jody could be that good looking and confident enough to wear a stylish sweater that not many men would be able to pull off.

As she was closing the register, she saw Joel crossing the street.

She went into the kitchen to grab the sandwiches out of the fridge, when the sight of Jody's sandwiches still there made her realize he had forgotten them. Taking them out, she went back out front.

She was pulling out her purse from under the counter when Joel came inside, carrying a cooler.

"Are you ready?"

"Yes." Sophie glanced down at the cooler. "I made sandwiches."

Joel's eyebrows arched. "That's a lot of sandwiches."

"They aren't all for us. Jody accidentally left his behind. I thought if we see him, we could give them to him."

"Accidentally? Sure, we can do that." Joel didn't sound happy.

"Is there a problem? I thought you and Jody are friends?"

"Jody and I have never had a problem before."

"Before? Did something change? Jody said you play video games together."

He gave her a half-smile. "Neither of us is used to losing."

Her expression cleared. "I see. Which one of you lost?"

Joel placed the sandwiches in the cooler. "No one yet. The game is ongoing."

"It must be a heck of a game." Picking up her purse, she came around the corner.

Joel had changed out of his uniform and was wearing a dark green button-down shirt and black jeans. He looked extremely attractive. The short sleeves of his shirt highlighted his muscles. Typically, she was more attracted to men who looked like Joel. He didn't have the perfection of Jody's features, nor was he as big as Jody. Joel would be a quarter-back, while Jody would crush anyone in his path.

Both types wouldn't have given her a second glance. She was flattered that Joel had asked her to go to the music festival, yet she couldn't help wondering: why?

Deciding to just enjoy the night, she let the thought slip away. Did it really matter why Joel had asked her out? She didn't want to overthink his intentions. It was just a date.

She locked the restaurant, and Joel escorted her to his car. When he held the door for her, she slid inside. Then Joel placed the cooler in the trunk while she put on her seat belt.

"Is the festival going to be crowded?" she asked once he pulled out onto the road.

"Everyone in Treepoint will be there."

"You didn't have to work?"

"No, I worked all the Christmas holidays. Greer is stuck having to work tonight."

Sophie didn't miss the satisfaction in his voice.

"Do you and Greer get along?"

"Put it this way—no."

Sophie laughed. "I have to admit, he takes getting used to."

Joel made a scoffing sound. "No one gets used to Greer; they just get tired and give in to him. Everyone in town jokes that he's going to live forever because when Death comes for him, Death will leave him behind because he doesn't want him in the afterlife."

She was wiping tears of laughter away when Joel found a parking spot. He hadn't been joking—the park was filled. The colorful array of blankets on the ground and the different-colored food carts had her itching to get out of the car. When was the last time she had done anything just for fun?

Getting out of the car when Joel opened the door for her, she blushed under Joel's appreciative gaze. He made her feel va-va, and by the end of the night, she hoped he lowered the voom on her, she inwardly cracked the joke.

If there was one guy in town who could keep her from making a fool out of herself, it was Joel. She wasn't naïve; she could see he was as much a player as Jody. There was one key detail that had her overlooking his past, though.

She wouldn't have to enter a rehab center to break her addiction to Joel, whereas she would with Jody. Catnip was addictive.

Chapter Twenty-Five

S ophie was on their date for twenty minutes before starting to wish she could go home. Joel talked incessantly about himself, and he didn't stop. He had talked about his childhood, and now he was on to his military career. She appreciated his service but didn't want to hear the gory details.

Listening to the music was the best part of being there. As she glanced around the crowd, she saw the Colemans sitting off to the side. They had backed up a truck, and Fynn was sitting on the tailgate with Isaac. The rest of their family were sitting on several blankets. Three coolers had been placed nearby. Not seeing Jody, she scanned the area and spotted him at the same time as Ginny.

She watched when a male singer stepped down from the stage before Ginny and Jody climbed up the steps. Jody held Ginny's hand protectively to make sure she didn't fall on the metal steps.

As Ginny walked to the microphone, Jody opened a case on the stage and took out a fiddle. The crowd started cheering before Ginny started singing.

She turned her head toward Joel. "Ginny's very popular here, isn't she?"

"She's popular everywhere," Joel told her.

Frowning, she thought back to when she had first met Ginny and remembered how she seemed familiar.

Before she could ask any more questions, Ginny started singing "I'll Fly Away," and Jody lifted the fiddle to his shoulder and started playing along. It was stirring hearing Ginny's melancholy voice as she sang while Jody kept up with her effortlessly.

"That was beautiful," she said softly when the song ended.

"You haven't heard anything yet."

Joel was right; Ginny sang another song that was much more modern, which she easily recognized.

"OMG!"

Joel started laughing at her reaction. "You didn't know?"

Sophie wanted to cry in embarrassment. She had a top-rated Indy singer working as a cook in her restaurant for free.

"Why on earth is she helping me out at my restaurant?" she asked, still in shock.

Joel only shrugged at her. "I've wondered the same thing myself. I don't think it's for the money. Not only did she make money singing until she stepped back from performing, but she makes big bucks songwriting. Her husband isn't hurting for money, either. He's one of the owners who are building that big housing development."

"This just gets better and better. I am so embarrassed. I can't believe I didn't recognize her."

"Why? Her hair color has changed, and you're used to seeing her in jeans and sweatshirts."

"I'm just surprised someone who is as popular as Ginny is also kindhearted. All of the Colemans are," she added.

Joel, who was taking a drink of his soda, started choking.

Sophie started patting him on the back. "You okay?"

146

"Yes ... it's just what you said about the Colemans. They aren't known for being kindhearted."

"They are to me." Glaring at him, she went back to listening to Ginny sing.

Sophie joined along, clapping with the others in the park when Ginny stopped singing.

Joel opened the cooler. "Hungry yet?"

"Yes."

He took out all the sandwiches.

"I should go take Jody's to him." Sophie prepared to get to her feet.

"Let me. Which ones are his?"

She was showing Joel when his cell phone started ringing.

"Excuse me." He answered his phone. From his expression, Joel didn't appear happy at being called.

"Can't you call someone else to work?"

She guessed they couldn't from the way Joel put the sandwiches back in the cooler.

"I'll have to cut our evening short. Baylin's ankle monitor is glitching, and I've been called in to make sure she's at her apartment."

She looked at Joel in surprise. "Baylin has an ankle monitor?"

"The sheriff made it a condition to keep her out of jail."

"But I didn't press charges."

"You might not have pressed charges, but Greer booked her on disorderly conduct, attacking a police officer."

"What did she do?"

"She ran a stop sign, and when Greer pulled her over, he smelled liquor on her and asked her to take a breathalyzer test. She attacked him."

Sophie almost didn't feel sorry for Baylin. Greer came into the restaurant daily, and there had been a couple of instances when she thought about attacking him, too.

She stood up to fold the blanket while Joel threw their empty soda cans away.

"Leaving already?"

Jody's voice had her lifting her head.

"Yes, Joel's been called into work," she explained.

"One of the hazards of dating a cop." Jody's eyes switched to Joel's.

"One of the benefits of working in a small town—it doesn't happen often."

Jody looked at the cooler as Joel picked it up. "Before you leave, you mind if I snag the sandwiches you made for me?"

"Of course not."

Joel opened the cooler, and Sophie reached inside to grab the sandwiches, then gave them to Jody.

"You know, if you want to stay, you're more than welcome to enjoy the music with my family."

"I couldn't ..." Sophie started to make an excuse.

"Sure, you can. Ginny could introduce you to everyone. You could even invite them for a drink at the restaurant to get them in the door."

Jody's suggestion was smart. She should take advantage of being at the festival to promote the restaurant. Her parents would be here next week. She would love for them to see how busy the restaurant had become.

"That's a good idea. Do you think Ginny would mind introducing me to some of the townspeople?"

"I think she'd be delighted."

Sophie smiled at Joel. "I might as well stay here. Thank you for bringing me. I had a good time with you."

"Me, too." Joel handed the cooler to Jody. "You might as well take this, too."

Jody took the cooler from him. "Thanks, Joel."

Sophie stared back and forth between the two men. "You

could always come back after you check on Baylin," she suggested.

The two men didn't break eye contact.

"I'm sure Greer will find something else for me to do."

Sophie gave Joel the blanket. "I'll see you later."

"Good night."

Jody held out his hand. "Sorry you were called into work. I'll make sure that Sophie gets back to her car."

"I'm sure you will."

Sophie turned her head to stare at Jody. "I think whatever video game you're playing is starting to affect your friendship."

"It isn't my call to end the game. Joel can stop it at any time."

Chapter Twenty-Six

J ody took his eyes off the road to glance in Sophie's direction. "Do you need your car? We're going to the same place, so you can ride in with Ginny in the morning."

Smothering a yawn with her hand, she answered, "I'm too tired to drive, anyway."

Jody felt her eyes on him in the darkness.

"You should be just as tired. You helped me finish cleaning the apartment last night and were at the restaurant at the same time as I was."

He kept his hands on the steering wheel despite how much he wanted to pull her close to his side and let her rest her head on his shoulder. This was the first time Sophie hadn't covered the exhaustion she must be feeling. The woman had to be surviving on fumes from the way she worked herself.

"I'm not going to disagree. I'll sleep well tonight."

"You're very talented at playing the fiddle. I didn't know people still played them."

"Not many do."

"How long have you played?"

"My dad tried to teach me before he died. After he passed, I started teaching it to myself. I wish I had taken playing more seriously before he passed away, but it makes me feel better that he'd be happy if he'd known."

"You were close to your father?"

"We all were. Dad could act like a kid as much as we were, yet you never forgot he was the parent. He didn't tolerate bullshit, believed in treating everyone the same, regardless of how much money they carried in their wallet, and was kind unless you showed him it wasn't reciprocated."

"He sounds like a good man," she said softly.

"He was," he agreed tightly. Missing his dad was a daily battle, for all of the family.

"I'm sorry you didn't get so fortunate with Marty."

Out of the corner of his eye, he saw her turn to stare out of the window.

"Me too," she said solemnly. "My father was just incapable of being close to anyone. I asked my mom once why she had married him. She said when they were dating, he treated her like a princess. After they were married, though, his behavior began to change. He wanted to keep her isolated. That's when she started working with him because he wouldn't stop badgering her until she did. She said it was the same thing after I was born—he didn't want anyone babysitting me while they were at work. That lasted until I was four." Sophie went silent.

"What happened?" he urged gently.

"I went into the kitchen when I wasn't supposed to, so Marty gave me one of his lessons not to do it again." Her voice was so low he had to strain to hear her. "Mom came into the kitchen and saw him. She picked me up and left. She divorced him after that. I only had to see him every other week for a few hours with supervision until after I turned eleven."

"I'm sorry."

"Nothing to be sorry about. Some people just shouldn't be parents. I think he hated me."

"If he hated you, then why did he leave the restaurant to you?"

"I have no clue. The only reason I can think of is Marty expected me to fail. He knew I had limited funds. He had made our lives a living hell. My parents and I moved from job to job, state to state, trying to stay ahead of him. I was able to save some money, so I guess he thought I would sink what money I had into the diner and be left with nothing."

"That's screwed up."

"You just summed up Marty."

Jody turned into the driveway, to the side of Silas' house, then turned off the engine. He felt her stiffen when he leaned toward her and gave her an amused glance as he opened the glovebox to take out a flashlight.

"I'm afraid I can't see in the dark."

Sophie gave an embarrassed laugh. "I can't either."

"Guess we're walking home together," he said before getting out of the truck to walk around and open her door. Jody took it as headway when she didn't pull away from his touch on her arm as they walked.

"I can't get over how large this property is."

"With all of our family, sometimes it doesn't seem large enough," he said wryly.

"I would love a family as large as yours."

"There's a way to get one for yourself."

"Oh no. I have to be perfectly content to have one or two children."

Jody shined the flashlight on the ground to the small path, which would lead to his trailer.

"I was thinking more that you could always marry into a large family. That would make them your family, too, wouldn't it?"

"True, if I like them."

"Do you like mine?"

He had to tighten his clasp on her arm when she stumbled.

"Oh, thank you."

He could feel her trembling as they neared the trailer.

"You didn't answer my question. Do you like my family?"

"Yes, I do. Well, here we are."

He nearly burst out laughing at the relief in her voice.

"Thank you for bringing me home. I had fun at the music festival. I'm glad you talked me into staying. Good night."

Jody continued walking her right up to the steps of the trailer. "Would you mind if I came in and grabbed a couple of my things?"

"I don't think that would be a great idea." Pulling her arm away from his touch, she started up the steps.

"Why not?"

Sophie turned around on the steps. "Jody, I'm smart enough not to open the door when a wolf wants to come inside."

He couldn't hold back his laughter. "You don't trust me?"

"I trust you."

"Then it's yourself you don't trust?"

Her face turned angry. "What's wrong, Jody? Shocked I'm the only woman in Treepoint who can resist you?"

"Prove it." He took a step forward, his hands going around her waist. "I've wanted you under me since you walked up to my table."

Sophie's hand went to his shoulder as if she was about to push him away. "I'm not attracted to you," she stated with seemingly angry certainty.

Jody didn't allow his hurt to show. "Like I said, prove it."

"If I do, will you accept I'm not and won't try again?"

"I will."

Sophie placed her other hand on his shoulder before pressing her lips to his. If he thought he would be able to remain unmoved while proving that she was attracted to him, he failed.

When her lips met his, he felt as if he had done a backflip off a diving board and didn't know which way was up when he'd hit the water. He might have let his cock overrule him into losing judgment a time or two, but he had never felt as if he had his legs swept out from under him.

Keeping his hands on her waist, Jody kept the kiss gentle, exploratory, holding the desire he was experiencing back. Her lips trembled under his yet yielded to the soft pressure, parting to allow his tongue entrance into her mouth.

Sophie might have allowed her mouth to part, yet she stood as still as a statue, her arms remaining on his shoulders. She wasn't into him.

Pulling his mouth away, he stared down at her.

"See? What did I tell you? Zip, zilch, nada. Friends now?" she asked him casually.

"You win, Sophie. Friends."

Chapter Twenty-Seven

Jody walked away from Sophie numbly. Instead of heading to Jacob's trailer, he walked toward Silas' house.

He didn't go inside; he went to the rise providing a clear view of the sky. Sinking down to the grass, he turned off the flashlight to stare up at the sky. Pinpointing the star he was searching for, he read the surrounding stars.

"I didn't see you here." Silas sat down next to him.

"Where did you expect me to be?"

"With Sophie."

"She wants to be friends and sent me on my way."

Silas' lips twitched in amusement. "I'm not used to you sounding so discouraged. She only met you a week ago."

"She's not attracted to me. I kissed her tonight, and she acted as if she would rather be doing her laundry."

"Ow, and you looked so nice tonight."

Jody turned his head to stare at his brother. "You can be a real dick when you want to be."

Silas' chuckle eased the hurt knot in his chest. "Jody, you were overconfident, and Sophie handed your ego back on a plate. I would have been disappointed in her if she had dropped to your feet and let you walk all over her like you have other women."

"I do not walk on women."

"Not literally, but you have become very spoiled. You're used to having it easy. Sophie isn't easy."

"No, she isn't. Sophie is nothing like I expected her to be."

"Don't lie to me, and stop lying to yourself."

"How am I lying to myself?"

Silas sighed, looking toward the sky. "Jody, we all loved Dad and Leah."

Grief welled inside of him.

"We all, in our own way, blame ourselves. Me for leaving to get the helmets, Ginny because it was her turn to ride the ATV, and you blame yourself for pestering Dad not to wait until I got back. Jody, you were just a kid, and kids pester their parents. It's the parents' job not to give in."

"Dad was a big kid himself. I had more sense than him," he said gruffly. "I'll never forgive myself."

"Ginny had to lay that blame to rest, and you have to, too. I'm not saying don't grieve them, but you can't keep self-sabotaging your life to pay them back for them losing theirs."

"I'm not," he protested.

"Aren't you? You were aware of your soul mate, yet you live fast and loose with other women, knowing it was inevitable your soul mate would find out. You losing your soul mate won't pay penance for Dad and Leah dying. Neither of them would want that for you. They both only want you happy."

Jody clenched his jaw to hold back the tears burning his eyes. "When"—his voice cracked—"will I stop missing them?"

"I can't give you an answer I don't know myself. I miss them just as much. There hasn't been a day that has gone by when I don't see Leah's face. I carried her on my hip when I had to get chores done, changed her diapers, tucked her in bed, taught her to read ..." Silas broke off. "Dad warned me that his death was near ... he didn't warn me that he would be taking Leah with him. He knew how much it was going to hurt me ... all of us.

"When I asked if there was a way to prevent his death, he told me he was ready to go. He had been without his soul mate too long, and she wasn't in this life.

"In our birthdate charts, Leah was the only one who didn't have a soul mate. I asked Dad about it, and he told me that she had just been born without one. I don't know if he had suspicions she would die so young. What he did say was this wasn't the only life we would have on earth. He said, when he died, he wasn't passing away; he was moving on to another life, to not be sad for him, but be happy for him."

"I don't know what true happiness is anymore."

"And you won't until you're willing to put the past behind you. Sophie is a smart woman. Could it be she senses you're not ready to give your heart to any woman? Her father taught her from an early age that men are deceitful. Show her the real Jody, that you're steadfast and loyal, and she won't be able to stop herself from falling in love with you."

Jody listened to Silas as he stared up at the sky. "If I show her the real me, she'll run."

Silas stood up. "Or she could surprise you. I think you're underestimating how strong Sophie is."

Jody heard Silas walk away, his mind going back to the day of the accident. He covered his face with his hands, trying to block out the image of Leah's happy face as she climbed onto the back of the ATV behind their dad.

Getting up, he started walking. Was Silas right? Was he self-sabotaging because he felt he didn't deserve to be happy? When he looked up, he found himself at the small family cemetery where Colemans had been buried for generations. Walking to the two graves that lay side by side, he stopped.

"I'm so sorry. I just wish I could talk to you."

"You have nothing to be sorry for and you know why you can't talk to them. Their souls moved on already."

Startled, Jody turned to the side to see Fynn walking toward him.

"Silas said he saw you walking in this direction." Fynn stopped next to him to stare down at the graves. "You weren't responsible for their deaths. Dad knew when I was born that Mother would not allow both of us to remain on earth for long. We would be too powerful. She was protecting Earth."

"How do you know?"

"I can see their past lives." Fynn looked around the cemetery. "We all are Mother's chessmen, to move or discard at her will. Anytime we get too strong or disobey her ... we are removed from the game."

"What reason did Mother have to remove Leah? She didn't have any gifts."

Fynn stared down at their sister's grave. "She was powerful. Dad tried to shield her, but Mother knew the power Leah would grow into, so"—Fynn snapped his fingers—"she was removed."

"Fynn, be careful ..."

"Why? Am I not being respectful enough?" Fynn gave a stark laugh. "Don't worry; she can't punish me by taking my soul mate. She's already accomplished that."

"Darcy is still young. She hasn—"

"Darcy isn't my soul mate."

Jody stared him blankly ... then it clicked with him. He had seen a huge behavior change in Fynn when ... "She was the girl killed on the school bus." Jody didn't know how to comfort his younger brother. "I thought Darcy was."

"No, she's Logan's."

Jody frowned. "You're trying to steal Logan's soul mate?"

"No, but if she likes me, I won't be pushing her away, either."

"Fynn, you can't destroy their lives. It will backfire. Bro, I'm paying for my mistakes. You can't read your future; the stars have been changing … Don't screw yourself over."

Jody felt a chill feather down his spine at the expression on Fynn's face.

Fynn must have seen his concern, because he went back to the brother he was more comfortable with, who had a loving heart.

"I won't. The only reason I said anything was because I didn't want you to continue beating yourself up. If you want to blame someone, blame Mother."

Concerned, Jody watched as Fynn left the cemetery. Then, looking upward, he went to his knees. "Forgive him. If you want to punish him, punish me instead."

Not expecting an answer, he rose from his knees only to find himself flung to the ground with such force the air was knocked out of his lungs. He had to lie there for several minutes before he could finally get his breath back. Managing to get to his knees, he looked back up at the sky.

"Gotcha. I'll mind my own business from now on."

Chapter Twenty-Eight

Carefully closing and locking the door, Sophie stepped back and placed a hand over her mouth. Her lips were still throbbing. The only way she had managed not to throw herself into his arms was the image of him carrying Baylin into her apartment.

The thought had been enough to let cold reason win the day. Complaining about it not being fair about how Jody affected her hormones, she went into her bedroom to take off her clothes. Naked, she went into the bathroom to take a shower. How much longer was she going to keep the façade of not being attracted to him?

Turning off the shower, she dried off then put on pajamas, then climbed into the bed. She turned off the light then rolled over to stare out the window, gradually feeling the tension leaving her body.

She should be proud of herself. She had placed Jody in the friendly zone and had made sure he wouldn't try to cross the line again. If she was so stinking happy she had won the challenge between them, then why was she regretting not inviting him inside?

What if, instead of winning, in reality, she was the loser?

Refilling a coffee cup for the customer at the front counter, Sophie watched as Jody took the orders of three women at a table in the middle of the restaurant.

"Can I get some cream?"

Sophie returned her gaze to her customer to find two sets of male eyes studying her. "Of course."

She went to the mini fridge behind her and took out a handful of creamers to give the men. Both were wearing Last Rider jackets. She hadn't been in Treepoint two days before finding out The Last Riders were a motorcycle club just outside of town.

The door opening had her turning her head to see Ginny's husband walk inside. Her jaw nearly dropped when she saw Gavin wearing the same black leather jacket. Staring, she watched as Gavin took a seat next to the men she was waiting on.

"Hello, Sophie."

"Gavin."

She was aware she was making a fool of herself for staring but couldn't help herself. When she had seen Gavin each time before, he was daunting. Sophie didn't think many people would be brave enough to take him on. In the Last Rider jacket and dressed in black, he was terrifying.

Forcing her vocal cords to work, she managed to ask him if she could get him anything.

"A coffee would be good."

The humor in his eyes eased some of the terror in her chest.

After making a cup of coffee, she turned back to the counter to find all three men focused on her.

"Sophie, these are some friends of mine." Gavin motioned to the man next to him. "This is Viper, the president of The Last Riders"—Gavin gestured toward the other man—"and this is Shade."

Sophie tried not look toward the cold-eyed man whom she had been avoiding the moment he had sat down. All three of them together chilled her to the bone.

"Nice to meet you both. Thank you for coming in. Can I get anyone anything else?"

"Sophie," Gavin's said in a hushed tone, "Viper wants to talk to you about your father."

She took a step back from the counter and came up against a brick wall. Startled, she turned her head around to find Jody behind her.

"Hear them out." Jody's hand went around her waist, urging her back to the counter.

Flustered at being so close to him, it took a second for her to concentrate on what Viper was saying.

"I wanted Reaper to introduce us so we could give you a heads-up about what your father was involved with in town."

"I really don't want to know what Marty was involved with."

"I don't blame you. I wish I could say the same. Unfortunately, Marty dragged us into his criminal enterprise, and we didn't know until it was too late. We still don't know all of the players involved. We're trying to weed them out as they become known to us."

"Weed them out?" she asked in a strangled voice.

Viper didn't bat an eyelash. "Report them to the police, naturally."

"Oh ..."

Report them to the police? she thought sarcastically. She would kiss Viper's ass if any official police reports had been taken from The Last Riders.

"I've already reported that a man contacted me the second day I opened the restaurant. He wanted two hundred thousand dollars that Marty owed him. He hasn't been back."

None of the men seemed surprised at the revelation.

"If he contacts you again, or anyone else does, give Shade a call, and he'll make sure you're protected."

The man seated next to Viper slid a plain card across the counter to her.

Sophie didn't reach out to take it. "I will after I make a report to the police."

Viper gave her a cold smile. "Whichever way you want to handle it is good with us. We've found, to our own loss, the people involved with Marty don't hesitate to hurt anyone getting in their way. Two of our club members were killed, and they nearly took out a woman and child belonging to another club member."

Sickened at what her father had been involved in, she picked up the card and slid it in the pocket of her apron.

"I apologize for the tragedy Marty brought to your club. I don't think any of his people will be back. I don't even have anything of his. The only thing he left me was the restaurant, and I cleaned this place from top to bottom—there's nothing here. I don't even know where he lived or where his belongings are, nor did he leave me any money in his will. So, you see, there is no reason for anyone to come here. I don't even know why the man did to ask me for the money Marty owed him."

Shade spoke for the first time. "If he came here, he came for a reason. Do you know anything else about your father's will?"

"No, but I can give you the name of the lawyer and his address." Sophie bent down to retrieve her purse. Searching through the contents, she pulled out the card and gave it to Viper.

"Thank you," Viper said, taking the card.

"Sophie, the customers are getting antsy."

Sophie nodded at Jody, seeing him holding out the ticket of the order he had taken.

"I better get busy." Excusing herself, she went to the kitchen, her mind in turmoil. Why would someone come to ask for such a sum of money? It would have been a foregone conclusion she would contact the police.

Ginny turned from the grill as she pulled out the hamburgers for her to fry.

"I just met a couple of your husband's friends."

"Really? Who?" Ginny peeked through the window looking out into the diner. "Oh, that's Viper and Shade. Mind keeping the eye on the grill for me while I go say hello?"

"Not at all. Go ahead. Take your time."

Putting the burgers on the grill, she thought again about calling her parents to stay in Arizona. They had already quit their jobs, given up the house they had rented, and loaded what possessions they had in their car. How could she tell them to wait?

She nearly burned the hamburgers and would have if Ginny hadn't come back in time. Ginny took one look at her and took over.

"What's wrong?" she asked, assembling the hamburgers.

"My parents. I don't know what to do. Should I tell them to stay in Arizona?"

Ginny looked at her curiously. "What brought this on?"

"What Viper said about Marty has me worried."

"What did he say?"

Sophie told her then said, "I'm worried about them coming here." She bit her lip. "What do you think?"

"Would you like me to ask Gavin for his opinion?"

Sophie nodded. Then she put two of the plates in the window and carried two out of the kitchen while Ginny followed behind her.

She left Ginny to talk to The Last Riders, and Jody, who was still standing at the counter, while she carried the plates to the table of women. Logan had come in to work while she had been in the kitchen and was waiting on a lone woman customer.

The women looked disappointed when she set the food on their table.

"Is something wrong with the food?"

One of the women tapped her nails on her glass. "Could you tell Jody we all need refills?"

The sound of the tapping was like the screeching of chalk on a board.

Sophie reached for the glass. "I'll take care of that for you."

The woman slid the glass away from her touch. "We'll wait for Jody."

"Certainly. I'll send him right over."

Reaching under the counter, she took out a plastic pitcher and shoved it into Jody's stomach. "Do you mind filling this up for me with ice and whatever those women are drinking?"

"Okay ...?"

Taking the two other plates out of the window, she nabbed the pitcher out of his hand just as he finished.

"I can take—"

"I've got this," Sophie cut him off.

The women looked angry when she returned with the pitcher and no Jody.

Setting the food and pitcher down, she glared down at the women. "Jody said he's busy, so he made the pitcher and told me to bring it here instead," she lied unrepentantly. "I hope that's okay?" she said with false sweetness. "If not, I can fire him on your say-so?"

"No! No!" the women hastened to assure her.

"We can see he's busy. We should have waited," the nail-tapper spoke for her group.

Giving them a curt nod, she averted her gaze from Logan's amused one to return to the counter.

Ginny had gone behind the counter, and Jody was cleaning the area they had been standing at.

He searched her face. "Is everything all right?"

"Everything's just fine and dandy," she snapped. "You know, I just noticed something."

Jody swiped a cleaning cloth over the counter. "What?"

"Most of my customers are women. I find that very interesting."

His eyes went toward the front of the restaurant. "So they are. I didn't notice, either."

Sophie gave him a dagger-sharp gaze. He returned it with innocent eyes.

"Does that bother you?"

"Why should it?" she gritted through clenched teeth.

Jody gave her a careless shrug. "No reason. Just asking."

She clenched her hands into fists to keep herself from snatching the cloth from him and using it to strangle him. "Do you mind refilling the iced tea dispenser for me?" By the time he finished, the women should be done eating.

From Jody's expression, he had gauged her motive. "Not at all." He gave her jaunty wink before moving around her, his shoulder accidently brushing against the side of her breast. "I'm always ready to satisfy a friend in need."

Chapter Twenty-Nine

Closing the drawer of the cash register, Sophie glanced out the window and saw Greer coming out of the sheriff's office. Curiosity held her in place when he walked to the side of the building, heading toward the parking lot. As he passed a car parked on the side of the road, he stopped and looked at it, bending down to examine the front tire. Rising to his feet, Greer went to his squad car and took something out of his trunk. Then he returned to the other car, and she saw he was filling the tire with air.

"What are you looking at?"

Sophie turned at Ginny's question.

"Nothing. Just being nosy."

Ginny smiled. "My favorite hobby. I didn't realize how much I missed interacting with people until I started helping out here."

"I don't know how I would have managed without yours and Jody's help. I talked to my parents and finally told them the situation here, like Gavin advised me to do yesterday. They decided they are still going to come here. They don't want me to be alone."

"I'm glad they're coming. I know you've missed them."

"I have." She frowned. "I'm still worried, but I'm hoping that I've seen the last of Marty's friends."

Ginny grimaced. "Me, too."

"The good news is when they get here, Jody and you won't have to help out anymore."

Ginny's hands went to her hips. "You're going to ditch me?"

Sophie could only gape at her. "I'm sure you have better stuff to do with your time."

"You're not going to get rid of me that easily. You're going to need a day off. You can't work around the clock, and I enjoy working here. I wouldn't even mind coming in a couple of days a week. You're going to need a life outside of the restaurant."

Folding her arms over her chest, Sophie stared Ginny down. "I know who you are, so why on earth would you rather be working here than being on a stage somewhere?"

"Because I enjoy working here. I hate performing."

Sophie didn't know how to respond to that. "Okay ... but if you get tired of it, just let me know. My feelings won't be hurt. Plus, I have enough to pay you, so you won't be working here for free anymore."

"I don't need the money. You can just give my wages to Logan."

"You're very kind, Ginny."

The door opening had both of them looking to see a woman enter. She gazed around the restaurant, and Sophie saw the expression on her face when she spotted Jody. The woman waved at Jody before taking a seat at one of the tables. Glumly, she straightened the condiment holder.

"I'm going to go bankrupt when Jody stops working here."

Ginny chuckled. "The ladies do love him."

"I wouldn't call them ladies with the way they act around him."

Dodging Ginny's amused gaze, she went to greet the customer, but Jody beat her to it.

"Hey, Jody," Sophie heard the woman practically purr as he approached her table.

Ginny rolling her eyes showed she wasn't the only one thinking that way.

"I need to find something to do in the kitchen before I gag."

A customer coming to pay kept her from escaping with Ginny. Staying behind the counter, she was treated to a birds-eye view of the woman flirting with Jody.

She wanted nothing more than to find Jody something else to do in the restaurant until the woman left, yet she didn't do a thing. Several times yesterday and today, she had used the play to keep him away from the various women who had come to the restaurant just to see him. She had passed irritated by ten this morning, and it wasn't even lunchtime yet.

Cool it, she told herself. What did it matter to her who flirted with Jody or if he flirted back?

Glancing at the wall clock, she counted how long Jody talked to the customer—six minutes. What was taking him so long to get her order?

Unable to resist glancing in their direction again, she saw the woman had placed her arm on the table and was sitting forward, her breasts resting on her arm.

Coming around the counter, she walked to an empty table where Logan had just removed the dirty dishes. She wiped the table down with a sanitizing cloth and was given the same view as Jody. Picking the cloth up in her hand, she strode back behind the counter to place it in the disinfecting solution.

She went to the glasses and filled one with ice and water before walking to the table where Jody stood.

"Jody, you should at least get your friend something to drink. With all the talking she's doing, she must be parched." Sophie met the woman's assessing gaze unwaveringly.

"Sorry," he apologized. "Chastity runs the children's boutique in town. She was asking me to tell Ginny and Alanna that she received a new shipment of clothes."

"I'm sure Ginny will be happy to hear that. Why don't you go tell her so she can come talk to her about them?"

"Sure."

Sophie didn't move away from the table. "Can I get you anything?"

"I'll take a salad to go. I'm afraid I've used too much of my lunchtime to eat it here."

"Which salad would you like?"

"Whichever is easiest for you to make. I'm flexible."

I bet you are, Sophie thought snidely.

Fortunately, Ginny reached the table.

She went to the kitchen to make a wedge salad in a carryout container, closing it when she was done. Dipping some blue cheese dressing into two small containers, she placed lids on them, grabbed a plastic bag, and carried it all to the woman's table, where she set them down.

Jody had made his way back to the table, joining the conversation with Ginny and Chastity.

"Here you go." Sophie gave her a smile. "Do you want to check it before I place it in the bag?"

The woman waved her away. "I'm sure it's fine."

It was the snotty way she talked to her that sent Sophie over the edge. Finding the opening of the plastic bag, Sophie shook it open, accidently knocking the still full glass of water over.

"You moron!" the woman hissed, standing up. Her beige silk top was soaked, as were the beige pants.

"I'm so sorry!" Sophie apologized insincerely. "At least it's just water. Your clothes should dry in no time."

"I'll get a towel." Helpfully, Ginny took off toward the counter.

Sophie was proud of herself until Chastity unbuttoned two more buttons on her blouse, exposing the lacy cups of her bra and the generous swells of her breasts to pluck several ice cubes out. Giving Jody a side eye, Sophie saw he was enjoying the view.

She maintained her composure and managed to hold it together as Ginny handed Chastity the towel and she jerked it out of her hand.

Sophie was moving before she realized what she was doing. She jerked it out of Chastity's hand just as rudely as she had done to Ginny. Smacking her in the chest with the towel, Sophie rubbed her chest roughly with it while at the same time pushing her back down into the chair. Chastity frantically tried to take the towel away.

"Ow, that hurts!"

Sophie removed the towel. "Sorry, I just didn't want you to catch a chill. I apologize for spilling the water. Of course, the salad is on the house."

Chastity shot up from the chair. "Keep the damn salad," she spat out, grabbing her purse and storming out.

Unconcerned, Sophie watched her leave. Then, picking up the salad and the glass, she turned to put them in the bus bin. Jody, Ginny, and Logan were all standing there, staring at her.

"What?" She frowned at the mixture of emotions on their faces.

Ginny started laughing so hard she had to sit down, Logan

took the towel to wipe up the water that had spilled with a wide grin on his face, and Jody looked dumbfounded.

Sophie took off toward the cleaning area then stopped to glare at Jody. "You might want to warn your friends that the next time I see them flashing their tits at you, they will be escorted out of the restaurant."

"To be fair, she wasn't flashing them until you dropped the water on her."

Sophie stared at Jody through slitted eyes. He was smart enough to take a step back.

"She was acting like she was on fire, so I put her ass out."

Chapter Thirty

She was sitting on the couch, blow drying her hair, when she heard a knock on the door. Turning the blow dryer off, she went to the door to crack it open.

"What do you want, Jody?"

"We need to talk."

The firm tone he used sent tingles down her back.

"Talk to me in the morning." She started to shut the door.

Jody put out a hand, grasping the door and preventing it from closing.

"I'm not dressed." Sophie used her weight against the door to prevent him from pushing inside.

"Go get changed. I'll wait here."

She could tell from his expression that there was no use arguing. Jody was determined to come inside. She could let him in, or he would come in regardless.

"Great," she told him sarcastically. "Give me a couple of minutes."

Jody removed his hand, allowing her to close the door.

She went to the bedroom and removed her nightgown to put on a pair of baby blue sweatpants. Not able to bear the thought of putting a bra back on, she chose a thick black sweatshirt. When she left the bedroom, she was tempted to lock the door and go to bed. If she wasn't certain he had a key to the door, she would have.

Sophie opened the door. "You can come inside." Folding her arms over her chest, she watched him. "I'm tired. I've been up since five and was about to go to bed. What was so important you wanted to talk tonight?"

Jody shut the door. "I want to know why you threw that water at Chastity?"

"I didn't. The bag hit the glass, and it spilled."

"You did it deliberately. You certainly didn't act upset that you did."

Sophie gave him a careless shrug. "I wasn't."

"So, it wasn't an accident?"

Stomping to a chair, she threw herself down. "Of course it was. Why would I deliberately spill water on her?"

"That's what I'm trying to figure out."

"Then you're wasting both of our time. It was an accident, plain and simple."

"I don't think it's simple at all. I think it was premeditated. I think you knew what you were going to do when you brought the water over."

Sophie laughed at him. "How was I supposed to know she was going to place a to-go order?"

"You would have found another way."

She rolled her eyes at him. "Why would I do that?"

"Because you were jealous," he said with raised brows.

"Over whom?" She deliberately played obtuse.

"Me."

"You're so full of yourself," she scoffed. "I wasn't jealous over you."

Jody's expression showed his disbelief. "If you changed

your mind about us being friends, all you had to do was say so."

She narrowed her eyes on him angrily. "I haven't changed my mind. As unbelievable as it sounds to you, I'm not attracted to you—I proved that to you."

"Yes, you did."

Her hands went to the arms of the chair, preparing to rise.

"Unfortunately for you, I can't say the same. I'm very attracted to you."

Shifting her gaze away from his, she lowered herself back into the chair. "So, you're reneging on our deal?"

"No, there's nothing wrong with being friends and lovers."

"You've made an art of doing that, haven't you?" she said snidely.

Jody tilted his head to the side, as if listening closely. "There it is again."

Confused, she frowned at him.

"The jealousy."

"I think it's time for you to leave."

Jody made no move to do so. "I'm not trying to be a nuisance, but we need to get this settled tonight, before you lose any more customers."

Sophie kept her face deadpan. "There is nothing to settle."

"I think there is. You just want to pretend that you're not attracted to me. I get that. You saw me with Baylin at the apartment, and then the next morning, I was cutting her loose. I can wish I were more like Matthew and not have to confess to being with other women, but I can't. What I can say is I didn't take what wasn't willingly offered."

"I bet you didn't," she said, unable to hide her disgust.

Jody's eyes narrowed on her. "Careful. People in glass houses shouldn't throw missiles."

Sophie shot up from the chair, clenching her hands. "What does that mean?"

Jody took a step forward. "It means, unless you're a virgin, don't condemn me for not being one."

"In this day and age, you're going to throw up my lack of virginity?"

"Only in regard to me not being one either."

Her jaw locked; she was determined to go to the bedroom and lock the door so she wouldn't have to continue the conversation. Unfortunately, Jody had roused her temper, and she was well past walking away.

Turning back to him, she stared at him in fury. "I don't live in a damn glass house," she snarled. "They're expensive. My house is made of bricks, so I can shoot as many damn missiles at you as I want. I've been too busy working since I was old enough to reach a busing station. Men don't normally go after women who look like me, especially when I keep my wallet and my thighs closed tightly. Men are predictable, if nothing else. When they can't get to one or the other, they stop returning your texts. I've never met a man whom I've come close to breaking my rules for."

His brow furrowed. "What rules?"

"Are you listening to me?"

"I think so. If you mentioned any rules, I think I would have remembered them."

"Let me make it easier for you. My rules are no cheating—"

"I've never cheated on a woman."

"Really?" Sophie gave him a satisfied smile. "Ginny told me all of her brothers have soul mates; did that include you?"

Jody hesitated, but he eventually answered. "Yes."

"Was Baylin, Mina, Chastity, or the numerous women you've been with your soul mate?"

His long pause was extremely gratifying for her. "No."

"You cheated on your soul mate with each of those women. You're a cheater. Strike one." Satisfaction poured out of her tone. "Rule two: he can't be too good looking."

"You're not serious?"

"I am. If they're good looking, nine of ten times, they're conceited. We know which side of that scale you fall on."

Jody didn't try to defend himself on that score.

"Rule three is for me rather than the man."

"Whew, that's a relief."

Sophie ignored the droll way he spoke.

"Rule three is to trust my instincts. Would you like me to tell you what my instincts are telling me about you?"

"Go ahead."

"My instincts are telling me not to take you seriously—you're only being helpful to lay the new girl in town." Condescendingly, she took a step toward him, no longer afraid of the feelings he aroused in her. How many times had she learned it was no use to run? Too many to count.

"I'm not blind to the friction between you and Joel. I'm not a naïve high schooler who is so impressed with the star footballers paying attention to her not to wonder why. I've lived in numerous states, worked in jobs where I came into contact with men daily, yet I've never had two extremely handsome men make a concentrated effort to spend time with me. I don't find that a coincidence. Do you?"

Chapter Thirty-One

Jody moved away from Sophie before he tried to shake some sense into the woman. Sitting down on the arm of the couch, he looked at her seriously.

"You're right on point with Joel. With me, you're wrong."

"I don't think so. Can I go to bed now?"

"In a minute, but you won't be going alone."

Sophie gaped at him.

Jody gave her a sensuous smile and stood up. He nearly smiled as she took a backward step away from him.

"Don't worry; I've never forced myself on a woman, and I don't plan to start with you."

"Then how do you plan to go to bed with me?"

"You'll invite me."

She laughed at him.

Jody ignored her laughter.

"You won't be able to help yourself, just as I haven't been able to help myself from wanting you. I have since the moment I saw you."

He should have realized her innocence from how embarrassed she became each time he mentioned his reaction to her.

"From what I see, you don't take having a soul mate seriously when it isn't convenient for you to have one. How many times have you used that excuse to party hearty, and then feel good about yourself when you walked away?"

He'd had enough of hiding the truth from her. Silas had advised him to be honest, to show her the real him.

"I'm your soul mate."

"I don't believe in soul mates."

"Let me say it another way that you can believe. You're mine."

She stared at him unblinkingly for so long that he was beginning to wonder what she was thinking. Then she unexpectedly went to the couch, picked up a throw pillow, and started hitting him.

He wished he had kept his mouth shut.

"I'm not yours, you big doofus. If I really were your soul mate, I would jump off a skyscraper!"

Jody tried to take the pillow away from her, only to find himself doubled over in pain, going to his knees. Grabbing his balls, he wanted to howl in pain, except he was in such excruciating pain he couldn't make a sound.

"Aw ... Does that hurt?"

Jody managed to open his eyes as she provoked him, knowing he was in too much pain to do anything about it.

"Do you still think I'm your soul mate?" Taunting him, she held the pillow like it was a baseball bat. "*You're mine*?" she mimicked him. "How many women have you used that line on?"

He thought it prudent to remain silent.

"Am I supposed to lie down and beg you to have sex with me?" The vindictive woman whomped him with the pillow as she screamed at him.

"I'm really starting to hate men. I had the worst father, whose idea of affection was to use a spatula when I did something he didn't like. If he wasn't enough of a prime example of mankind, I met Kirk, who acted like he really cared for me until we went out on a third date and he ditched me at a steakhouse, leaving me to pay for an expensive meal. If that wasn't enough, I met Jorge. He was a *real* winner ..."

Jody guessed he wasn't from the scorn-filled voice that was shouting at him.

"He stole my car on our first date. Mark was almost as bad. When I didn't have sex with him on our first date, he sent me a text saying I was too ugly to fuck, anyway."

She bopped him on his shoulder when she walked around him. "I'm not a fool! You were flirting with Chasity! I have glasses. She practically stripped to show you her tits!"

"I was not flirting with her," he said hoarsely.

That earned him another bop.

"Don't lie!" she screeched louder at him.

She went to the door and slid on her flip flops before coming back to him to whack him with the pillow. "I'm going for a walk, and when I get back, you better be gone!"

Jody had had enough. Before she could draw back, he grabbed her by the wrist to pull her down onto the floor.

Pure hell broke loose.

Sophie leaned forward and bit him on the shoulder.

"That hurt, Sophie!"

"Good! I was trying to!"

"I like it."

Pressing his mouth to hers, he swept his tongue inside, giving her a passionate kiss. Expecting her to bite his tongue off, he groaned when she responded just as heatedly.

His hands went underneath her shirt, needing to feel her skin. He pulled his mouth back as he glided his hands upward to cup her bare breasts. "You belong to me."

"Shut up."

He stared at her with grim intensity, tightening his hands on her breasts. Hearing her gasp, he lowered his mouth to hers again as he circled her nipples with his thumbs. He used his shoulders to push her to the floor. Biting down on her bottom lip, he notched his cock against her groin, then slid his hands out from under her top and pulled it over her breasts. He could still see his handprints on her creamy flesh. Jody removed his teeth from her lip, enjoying seeing the slight contour.

"You make me as hard as a rock."

Sophie gave a shuddering whimper, which had him rising off her to jerk her pants off.

"Jody ..."

His hand went to her pussy, finding her damp. "Your little clit is begging to come out and play."

Twirling his finger over her clit, he moved back between her thighs to suck it into his mouth. Sophie nearly jumped off the floor. Able to hold her in place with his hands on her hips, he used his tongue to play with her, tasting her as she became wetter.

He groaned in satisfaction when her thighs clenched around his head as her hips twisted beneath his mouth.

"That's it, baby. You're going to come for me, aren't you?"

Gliding his tongue down, he slid it inside of her, exploring, before pulling back to return to her clit. He bit down gently and felt her give a little shudder as she orgasmed under his mouth.

Jody didn't give her time to recover before he raised himself over her to kiss her until she was gasping for air.

Reaching for the pillow she had been hitting him with, he raised her up enough to slide it under her ass. "Are you comfortable?"

Sophie lifted glazed eyes to his. "Huh?"

His mouth went to her neck. "I asked if you were comfortable."

"Yes ..."

Jody smiled into her neck when she trembled as he sucked.

"You're a very passionate woman, Sophie. Be very grateful you saved yourself for me."

She stiffened under him. He could tell she was about to take umbrage against him for her being a virgin.

"You hit me again, I will pay you back."

His hands went to her ass, lifting her slightly as he sucked harder on the flesh in his mouth. While thrusting his cock inside of her in small increments, he gradually sucked on her harder. Jody could feel her pussy grow wetter. Her moans had him wanting to pound his dick into her, but he held his own desire back as he inched his cock forward.

Her wiggling hips nearly dislodged him.

Going to his knees, he used his hands on her hips to pull her upward at the same time he sat down, pulling her onto his lap. His cock pierced through her hymen in one swift movement.

Jody clamped his mouth over hers at her scream.

"Give it a minute, baby. I'm going to make it feel good for you." He used his hands on her hips to set her down on his cock. "Lift your tit to my mouth."

At her pained expression, he lowered one hand from her hip to play with her clit. "That better, baby?"

She gave a hesitant nod.

"You can wiggle on me all you want in this position," he urged her.

"I don't want to."

"You'll get used to having me inside of you."

He wanted to laugh at her expression. Sophie was good at hiding her passionate nature. Jody blamed Marty for that habit. She had been trained to be docile and behave to keep her from getting a babysitter. The son of bitch was lucky he was dead.

"I want that tit."

Removing a hand from her hip, he smacked her on the ass.

Startled, her eyes met his.

He watched for her reaction and gave her a stern frown when he saw only arousal in hers.

"Arch your back."

She arched her back.

Taking a rosy nub between his teeth, he tugged on it while his hand went back to her hip to move her over his cock. Her pussy gradually accommodated his cock, and she could move over him easily.

Grinding her against him, he released her nipple to roll the thick nub over the roof of his mouth.

Jody heard her give another scream as she orgasmed again.

Laying her back on the floor, he released his pent-up passion and pounded inside of her as he spread her legs wider, determined to reach as deep as he could inside of her.

The way she looked touched him. She seemed so vulnerable.

"Am I hurting you?"

"No, it feels good."

He could barely hear her soft reply.

"Do you want more, or do you want me to stop?"

"There's more...?"

Jody had to grit his teeth at her innocent reply.

"Before the night is over, I'm going to know your body better than you do, and when I do ... you can get started on mine."

Chapter Thirty-Two

Sophie carefully left the bathroom after managing to get dressed. Holding a bottle of Tylenol in a death grip, she glanced toward the bed, seeing Jody was still sound asleep. He was lucky she didn't smother him before she managed to crawl out of the bed.

Every bone in her body hurt. She had thought she was in good physical shape until she had spent the night engaged in a sexual marathon with him.

Yawning, she poured herself a glass of orange juice to take the pills.

When she heard the bedroom door open, she turned to find Jody walking out, completely naked.

"You should get dressed!"

He raised a brow at her.

Taking the glass from her, he slid an arm around her waist.

"Why? It's just the two of us."

"'Cause ..." She flushed, unable to come up with a plausible reason other than it was hard to look at his dick without feeling a heated warmth spread through her body.

"Do whatever you want," she mumbled, taking the glass back to pour some juice.

"I will." His hand went to the nape of her neck as he pressed a kiss to her cheek. "Good morning."

"Good morning."

She managed to sit, unable to meet his eyes for long. She moved away to put on a light sweater.

"Why are you leaving so early?"

"Ginny taught me how to make biscuits yesterday. I want to get there early enough so I can make them. She's not able to come in this morning; her daughter caught the bug Freddie had."

"Give me ten minutes, and I'll come in with you."

"No, you don't—"

"I don't have to. I want to. I don't want you going out so early alone. I won't take long."

She was tempted to leave while he was getting dressed. How could she still want him after spending the night with him? She felt as if having sex only increased her appetite for him.

Inwardly, she groaned. She had known the man was catnip. She should have closed the restaurant and sold it the first day he had come inside.

"It wouldn't have mattered."

She was so focused on her thoughts that she hadn't heard him reenter the room.

"You don't know what I was thinking."

"You're already regretting last night."

Sophie turned to place the glass into the sink.

Coming up behind her, Jody slid his arms around her waist.

"I don't want to talk about last night."

She felt him laugh against her back.

Straining against him, she turned around in his arms. "I hate you."

His expression turned serious. "No, you don't. You wish you did, and that makes you angry. I'm not your shining knight, and you resent that. I might not be a chaste knight, but I have other virtues that are just as important. I'm loyal to those I love, I'm strong enough to protect those I do, and I don't shirk from doing what needs to be done."

"You're also not shy."

Jody chuckled. "No, I'm not. Give me a couple more nights, and you won't be either."

Glowering at him, she shoved him aside to move toward the couch. "If you're going with me, you better hurry, or I'll leave you," she threatened.

"Yes, ma'am."

Sophie tried not to look at his naked backside as he walked to the bedroom but failed miserably. She was still debating her sanity when he came back.

"Ready?" he asked, pulling on a thin jacket.

"Where did you get the clothes? You weren't wearing those last night when you came over."

"I have of box of clothes under the bed."

Sophie stared at him suspiciously. "Isn't that convenient."

"Yes, it is." He grinned, going to the door.

When she didn't rise from the couch, he looked at her curiously. "Ready?"

"Yes." Pressing her lips together to prevent herself from grimacing, she used the arm of the chair to get to her feet.

"Sore?"

Expecting to see him gloating, she saw he was frowning in concern instead.

"A little," she admitted, forcing her legs to move.

"You can't work like this."

"Watch me."

"I don't think so. You need a hot bath to loosen your muscles."

"In case it escaped your notice, you don't have a bathtub."

"No, but Jacob has a hot tub."

"I'm not going to Jacob's to get in his hot tub."

"Why not?"

"Because I'm going to work."

Jody blocked the door. "Not until you get in the hot tub."

"I'm not going—"

"Do you have a swimsuit?"

"No."

"I'll call Ginny and see if she has a spare one."

"Don't you dare!" she yelled when he reached for his cell phone.

"I won't wake her up. Gavin's probably awake; he can get it for me."

Sophie buried her face in her hands. "I don't want them to know you spent the night here."

At his silence, she peeked through her fingers to see his abashed expression.

"They already know," he admitted.

Her hands dropped. "How would they know?"

"I'm sure they heard you yelling last night. You made a hell of a ruckus."

"Please tell me you're joking?"

"Maybe not all of them heard, but Jacob and Isaac did. And, knowing them, they told the rest of the family."

Sophie wanted to lie down and die.

She started looking around.

"What are you looking for?"

"My pillow."

Chapter Thirty-Three

Sophie took a bite of the roast beef on her plate as she listened to the conversation at the table. She shot a sharp glance at Jody when he placed an arm on the back of her chair, but he only scooted his chair closer to her. He was making it plain to his family they were a couple before she was ready to admit it to herself.

He was pushing every boundary she had for herself. He wouldn't stop until she got in the hot tub this morning, nor would he take no for an answer when he wanted her to close the restaurant early so they could have dinner with his family.

What made her more wary was she had given in both instances.

"Have you heard anything from the school yet?" Silas asked as he passed the rolls.

"No," Alanna answered, pulling her hair from her toddler's sticky grasp. "They probably won't contact me until they start filling vacant teaching positions."

Matthew's wife was pretty and had made her feel comfortable when they first met. She had the same friendly attitude Ginny had shown her.

Alanna caught her staring at her. "Feeling overwhelmed?"

"No," she admitted. "I was just thinking how kind everyone has been to me. I would have left Treepoint if not for your family. I'm very grateful to all of you."

Alanna gave her a sweet smile. "I haven't done anything."

Sophie shook her head. "You babysat Ginny's children so she could help me at the restaurant. The good news is my parents should be here tomorrow, and you all can get back to your normal lives." Seeing the way Ginny looked at her, she added, "At least not so often. Ginny is determined to keep working full-time."

"At least until she gets pregnant again. Then she won't be able to. She gets terrible morning sickness," Fynn said matter-of-factly as he buttered his roll.

Sophie looked at Ginny questioningly.

"Don't worry; that won't be happening anytime soon."

"October."

Sophie turned her eyes back to Fynn, catching the warning glances his family was giving him.

"Am I missing something?" she came out and asked, getting a weird feeling.

"No, Fynn is a budding astrologer," Silas explained, cutting the tension in the room. "It's a hobby of his."

"That's interesting. What brought about your interest in astrology?" she asked, taking another bite of the beef.

"Our father had a deep interest in astrology and passed it along to all of us," Silas answered for Fynn.

"Is that why you all believe in soul mates?"

Despite Jody telling her that she was his soul mate, she still believed it was a bunch of malarky.

"Yes." Silas placed his fork down on his plate. "I take it you don't?"

"No."

"I understand. Most people don't."

Alanna gave her a smile. "I didn't believe it at first, either."

"You do now?"

"Oh, yes. I can't imagine my life without Matthew, and I won't have to. It's very comforting to me that our souls are linked."

"Let's see if you can say the same thing when you've been married forty years." Isaac laughed. "You'll be searching for a chainsaw to cut the link between you guys by then."

The table broke out in laughter. Alanna laughed along with the others at the dirty look Matthew was giving Isaac.

After dinner, they sat in the living room while the children played. Sophie couldn't help but notice the teenager Ginny had brought with her. Lennon was sitting on the floor, playing with the children. The girl appeared to be sixteen or seventeen, was very pretty, and she hadn't spoken a word when Ginny introduced her. While Lennon was helping set the table, Ginny had explained she was a friend of the girl's foster mother, and Lennon stayed at Ginny's house during school breaks.

Gavin seemed tolerant of the girl and didn't seem upset she stayed close to Ginny's side.

While she enjoyed listening to the banter going back and forth between the siblings, she continued watching the kids play.

Alanna sat Alex down on the floor. The adorable baby, who was a miniature version of his father, was shoving one fist in his mouth while attempting to maintain his balance. Ginny's daughter, who was playing with blocks, handed one to Alex, which he promptly dropped. Leah reached out to pick the block up, and as she did so, Alex reached out to grab Leah's hair. The little girl giggled, reached out to take the baby's hand, and then Sophie jumped when Leah started howling in pain, holding her hand.

Ginny, Reaper, and Silas simultaneously went for Leah. Gavin reached her first.

"Give her to me."

Sophie was shocked at the way Silas ordered Gavin to give his own daughter to him.

Ginny was trying to grab Leah's hand, which she was holding close to her chest, which made Leah cry louder.

Ginny looked away from Leah to Silas, who had his hands out with a curious expression on his face.

"Give her to him, Gavin."

Hearing the urgency in his wife's voice, Gavin reluctantly handed Leah over. Gently taking Leah into his arms, Silas started crooning to the upset child, turning around to walk into the dining room. Everyone anxiously watched the two.

Glancing down at the children on the floor, Sophie saw Alex was crying, frightened by Leah's cry. Big fat tears were rolling down his cheeks.

Seeing everyone's attention centered on Leah, Sophie leaned forward to pick the baby up. Her movement caught Alanna's eye.

"No! Don't touch him."

Matthew hurried over to scoop the crying child into his arms.

"I'm sorry, I just—"

Alanna shook her head. "There's no need to apologize. I didn't mean to yell at you. It's just ..." Alanna seemed to be at a loss of words to explain her outburst.

"Alex doesn't know you well, and being touched by a stranger could have set him off crying louder than Leah," Matthew explained, patting his son on his back.

Sophie glanced back over at the other child, seeing Silas handing her back over to Gavin. Leah had stopped crying and was snuggling into Gavin's chest. Gavin had a fearsome appearance, yet the sight of him gently rocking his daughter brought a lump to her throat

Gradually, the room went back to normal with conversations starting again, yet Sophie noticed Matthew or Isaac kept Alex with them rather than letting him play with Leah or Freddie again.

Alanna moved to the couch where Gavin and Ginny had taken a seat after putting Leah back on the floor to play with the block. Sophie wished she could overhear what they were talking about. Alanna seemed to be tearfully apologizing.

She started to go over there to tell them Alex had done nothing wrong—he had barely touched her when she had started crying.

Jody took her hand, stopping her.

"Let's go for a walk. I need to walk dinner off."

"Okay, I just need to speak to Ginny and Alanna before I go."

"Leave it alone." Jody tugged her to her feet. Without giving her a chance to say good night, he ushered her out the door.

Sophie gave him a curious look as he closed the door behind them. "What's the rush?" she asked. "I was just going to explain what happened. Alex barely touched her. I don't know what set Leah off, but Alex didn't hurt her. Alanna is upset, thinking he did—"

"No one is angry at Alex. Let's take that walk. You need to loosen up your muscles."

Blushing at the way he was looking at her, she went down the steps. Having never been in an inner circle of a family before, she assumed she was making more out of it than the weirdness she had felt.

"I shouldn't have tried to say anything. I'm glad you stopped me. I forgot my place."

Jody frowned at her. "What place?"

"I'm not a member of the family."

They continued walking. Jody showed her the different areas of their mountain she hadn't seen before. He took her into the building where Matthew and Isaac had their forge, where they made their fencing materials. Leaving the building, they walked until they had to go down a deep trail to where Silas kept the animals. Jody also showed her the storage buildings, which were like small grocery stores that held all of their supplies.

Sophie stared around the building in awe. "One thing's for sure: we have an apocalypse, you guys are good to go for at least a couple of years."

Jody laughed. "Maybe a year, with as many mouths to feed as we do. Silas intended to buy a couple of calves to raise to slaughter, but when Matthew and Alanna got together, he changed his mind."

"Why?"

Jody took her hand as they left the storage building.

"Alanna gets too attached to the animals. It's easier to buy from a farm that Silas goes to rather than upset her."

"I saw her eating dinner—she's not a vegetarian."

"She's not. She just doesn't want any of the animals she named sitting on the dinner table."

After showing her Moses and Matthew's home, he took her to a small creek.

"This area is beautiful. I'm surprised no one has built their home here."

Jody dropped down onto the ground near the creek. Taking his cue, she sat down next to him.

"We don't want to spoil the natural beauty here. Freddie left each of us a section of land. This is Silas'." Jody pointed to an area close to the road that led to the back road. "It extends to the main road."

Sophie looked at him in surprise. "I thought the main

house was Silas'.'"

"No, the house belongs to Fynn.

"There's another section that is undeveloped, which belongs to Ginny. She was building a house there when there was an explosion, and it was destroyed. Silas let Ginny have the land that would have been Leah's if she had lived."

"Who will get Ginny's original property, then?"

"Silas will make the decision. It will go to one of the children when they grow older. The land will remain in the Coleman family regardless of whom he gifts it to."

"Your family has made yourselves self-sufficient."

"Which was our ancestor's intention. Dad and Silas have turned down numerous offers to sell."

"I'm glad. Places like this are hard to come by."

Sophie watched curiously as Jody removed his shoes and socks, placing his feet onto the grass. "What are you doing?"

"Grounding myself. Have you heard of it?"

"I have. I've just never actually seen anyone do it."

"The beauty is it's not hard to do." Reaching out, he took off her shoes and socks, then placed her bare feet back on the grass. "Now you're grounded."

They sat quietly. Sophie had never felt so relaxed. The night before and getting up early was catching up to her. She didn't want to leave the tranquil spot, yet she couldn't help becoming drowsy.

Jody stretched out his legs. "You can lay your head on my thigh," he offered.

Sophie took his suggestion, feeling strange at the new experience of being with a man she didn't feel uncomfortable with as she drowsily closed her eyes. Shifting into a more comfortable position, she then opened her eyes. Groggily, she thought the grass was bending toward her and Jody, as if each blade of grass was reaching for them. Thinking she was imagining what she was seeing, she closed her eyes and fell asleep.

Chapter Thirty-Four

Checking to see if Sophie had fallen asleep, Jody ran a finger down her cheek. When she didn't move, he waved at Moses, who was carefully camouflaged behind a tree. He watched his crouching brother palming the earth from afar, directing the ground to send electrical waves to repair Sophie's muscles. Like Jacob had done for her in the hot tub.

He reached for his cell phone, careful not to wake her.

Is Leah all right? he texted Silas.

Yes, she was slightly burned. Alex's gift is appearing much sooner than Matthew's. He will have to be watched closely until he can learn control. Did Sophie see anything?

No.

You need to tell her. With her living here, it is only a matter of time before she finds out.

I will. I just need to get her to the place where I can tell her.

When will that be?

After I know she loves me.

Ending the text, he gazed up at the sky. It was getting dark.

Gently, he called her name, then saw her eyes open behind her glasses.

"Did I sleep long?"

"About thirty minutes. I don't like being this close to the creek at night. There are several wild animals in the woods, and I don't want to take a chance staying any longer out here with you."

After they put their shoes back on, Jody helped Sophie to her feet.

They had only walked a couple of minutes before Sophie started walking faster.

"I must have needed that nap. I'm not as stiff as I was before."

Sliding his hand from her lower back to her ass, he shot her an intimate glance. "I'm glad."

Smacking his hand away, she started to put distance between them. Jody grabbed her hand and pulled her back to his side.

"I'm afraid you'll fall in the dark."

"Then keep your hand away from my butt."

"Yes, ma'am. I promise to keep my hand away from your ass when we're out in public, unless I have your permission."

"I wouldn't exactly call this public."

"Does that mean I can touch your ass anytime I want to?"

"No, it does not."

When they reached where they needed to veer off onto the trail leading to his trailer, he glanced up at the darkened sky. His heart lurched in his chest at what he saw.

As he hurried Sophie toward his trailer, he tried not to make it obvious he was rushing her, but fear was pounding in his chest.

Relief filled him when the trailer came into sight.

At the trailer door, he waited for Sophie to open it then turn the light on. When she turned back to him standing outside the door, he could tell she didn't want him to stay. Saved from having to make an excuse, he pressed a quick kiss to her lips.

"Good night. Make sure you lock the door."

If he weren't so worried, he would have laughed at the consternation on her face. He had burst her bubble of shooting him down. Jody would be back once he talked to Silas about what he had seen in the stars.

He came out of the trail to meet a waiting Moses, and they started walking toward Silas'. He glanced up at the stars and grew more concerned.

When he passed Matthew's large truck, he saw his other brothers were already outside, looking at the sky. Their expressions mirrored his fear.

Matthew noticed his arrival and moved closer to Isaac, leaving him a space empty next to Silas.

"Does Fynn know who it is?" he asked Silas.

Grimly, Silas shook his head.

"Why are we allowed to see the death star covered in blood and not know which star it will destroy?"

"Dad always said our gifts are a double-edge sword," Silas murmured. "Dustin called and said Logan won't be in to work tomorrow. He warned us to stay close to the mountain."

"You tell Ginny she won't be going to the diner tomorrow?"

"She said if you can keep Sophie home, she will, too."

Jody already knew how that suggestion would go.

"Sophie won't stay home."

"Figures." Silas turned a troubled expression toward him. "Why is nothing ever easy?"

"I wish I knew," he said somberly. "I guess it will be just as useless for me to ask you to stay here tomorrow?"

"I can't let her go alone."

"She won't be alone—Reaper will be there. Greer will be on the alert, and I'll help if needed—"

Jody turned to him sharply. "You stay on the mountain. I don't want you to jeopardize your happiness for us anymore. We're all grown men, and we have to fight our own battles away from the mountain. You've done more than your fair share."

"When you have children, you're going to discover parents can't be happy until their children are."

Jody had to hold his emotions back at Silas' words. From his brothers' expressions, the meaning had hit them the same way.

"We love you, too."

All of them resumed staring up at the sky.

Moving to where Fynn stood by himself, Jody studied his profile in the light the porch gave off.

"If you're going to ask me who it's meant for, save your breath. I don't know."

"I'm more concerned with you tonight than what could happen tomorrow."

Fynn dropped his eyes to his. "Why are you worried about me?"

"We are here for you, Fynn. If your gifts are making you unhappy, stop using them, ignore them."

Fynn gave him a wry smile. "How am I supposed to stop?"

"Stop looking to the stars. You don't use your gifts when you go to school; just do the same here. Eventually, it'll become second nature."

Fynn continued to look at him. Then his eyes moved to their brothers, who were listening. Each of them had made the same decision that Fynn needed to make.

"You don't need to make the decision tonight. Think it over. You said you lost your soul mate, that she's no longer there. I think she is, or Dad wouldn't have put her on your chart. Mother made sure we can't see our future, and as much as I complain about it, I see why. She is our ruler, and she wants our loyalty, regardless of what we would prefer to do. Yet, as queen, she is also our Mother and seeks to protect us. She may show you parts of the future, but the future can change at any time by our actions. She set us on a path where she can watch and care for us. Until we break from that path, she cannot protect us if we're not supposed to be there in the first place."

"Then why are you going to town tomorrow?"

"I am loyal to my queen, but I have a duty to protect my woman."

Jody stayed an hour, planning where each of them would be stationed on the property in case the unexpected happened and the death the bloody star was forewarning about could take place on the mountain. Here, they were given free rein to use their powers, unless it involved healing physical wounds of someone meant to be taken.

Saying good night to his brothers, he made his way to his trailer. She wouldn't be happy to see him again tonight, but he was going to have to convince her to let him stay.

Despite being confident he could protect Sophie from what was going to happen tomorrow, he had a feeling of dread, as if the electrical currents flowing through the earth were warning him.

Sophie answered the door on his first knock. "Why am I not surprised?"

Jody grinned at her sarcastic expression. "I couldn't sleep."

"Call Ginny and ask her to borrow one of Leah's teddy bears."

"Are you going to make me sleep with Jacob? His snoring keeps me up all night."

"Will you sleep on the couch?"

"I'd rather sleep with you." Jody reached out, sliding his

hand around the back of her neck. "I can sleep on the couch if you make me. How about if I promise just to hold you, would that work?" Letting his fingers caress her skin, he stared at her soulfully. "I need you tonight, baby. Any way I can get you, I'll be content."

Conflicting emotions crossed her face before she opened the door. Once he was inside, she locked the door after him.

"What were you doing?"

"I was going to bed."

Jody looked at the couch unhappily. "Where am I sleeping?"

"On the couch. You know where the blankets are. Good night."

He gave her a pouting face as she went to the bedroom, then moved to the small chest against the wall, where he kept extra blankets and pillows for when one of his brothers spent the night.

After placing the pillow and blanket on the couch, he went to the wall to turn off the overhead light. He sat down and removed his shoes and clothes before lying down on the couch in his underwear, pulling the blanket over him. Rolling over to face the bedroom door, he closed his eyes.

He was almost asleep when he heard the bedroom door click open. He opened his eyes and saw Sophie's shadow crossing the floor toward him to stand over him.

"I hate myself." Self-loathing filled her voice.

"Why?"

"I shouldn't want you, but I can't make myself stop wanting you."

He made no move to rise from the couch. "You shouldn't hate something that isn't in your control," he told her as if they were discussing an everyday topic. "You can't fight what's between us, because it's not your conscious mind or body you're fighting against. Our souls are two parts of a whole. I have half; you have the other half. They were meant to be together.

"I can't make you believe you're my soul mate. I could take a lie detector test right in front of you, and if I were asked if I ever thought a woman I have been with was my soul mate, I would say no. If I were asked if you were my soul mate, I would say yes. I would even throw in an extra question for you. Do you love Sophie? I would say with every part of my being."

"You haven't known me long enough to love me," she whispered in the dark.

"I might have only met you recently in this lifetime, but I've loved you for eternity."

Jody saw her hand reach out in the darkness. "I'm a fool to believe you."

He picked her up into his arms. "You're nobody's fool."

Chapter Thirty-Five

"I'm going to have to buy a hot tub if you're going to keep spending the night," she groaned. A one-hundred-year-old woman could get out of bed easier than her.

Jody laughed as he walked out of the bathroom, zipping his jeans. Seeing that, she wanted to lie back down and beg him to take her again.

She was sick. How in the world could she still want to make love to him as sore as she was? Forcing her legs to move, she glared at him.

"What did I do?"

"Don't give me that innocent face. I wouldn't be this sore if you hadn't come back last night."

"What's the fun in that?" he teased.

"Any more fun, and I will be in the hospital." She moaned in pain as she went into the bathroom, slamming the door behind her.

"You're sleeping at Jacob's tonight!" she yelled from behind the closed door. Her shoulders slumped when she heard him laughing.

"You deserve to be miserable. You shouldn't have opened the door," she told her reflection in the mirror.

Removing her robe, she stepped into the shower and stayed under the water much longer than she should have if she was going to open the restaurant on time. Finally, she turned the water off and got out.

When she opened the bathroom door after toweling off, she was relieved to see Jody had left the bedroom.

Dressing, she reminded herself that she needed to wash clothes if she was going to have a clean top tomorrow.

She left the bedroom once she had brushed her hair and saw Jody had prepared each of them a mug of coffee.

"Thank God." Pausing by him, she pressed a kiss to his mouth. "And you, of course."

"You aren't mad at me anymore?"

"No, the steam from the hot water must have melted most of it away."

Picking up the mug, keys, and purse up from the table, she headed for the door.

"Let's take my truck. There's no use for both of us driving into town."

"Are you sure? What if my parents make it to town early? I won't want to come back here immediately. You might be stuck in town until late."

"You don't want me meeting your parents?"

She could give him an answer immediately. Her parents wouldn't be happy she had become involved with Jody so quickly. She had mentioned the Colemans when she talked to them each night without talking about Jody in particular.

As she got in Jody's truck, she saw his attention on the sky.

"Are you into astrology, like Fynn?" she asked once he was inside.

"Somewhat."

Starting the truck, Sophie could see his expression when the dashboard lit up.

"When we get home tonight, we need to have a talk."

Sophie looked away from him. Here came the part she had seen coming—he was going to tell her that he had been mistaken about her being his soul mate.

Fighting back tears, she turned her head to look out the window so he couldn't see she was upset.

"Scoot over here."

"What?"

Jody brought the truck to a stop before entering the main road. "I said, unbuckle your seat belt and slide over here next to me."

His gentle voice had her following his directions.

Unbuckling the seat belt, she slid across the bench to sit next to him, then found the middle seat belt and buckled herself back in. Once she was settled, he pulled onto the road.

His hand went to her thigh. "I want to talk about our future tonight. I don't want to wait months for me to propose to you. I want us to get married."

Her eyes flew to his face. "You're kidding."

"I'm serious. I didn't want to propose this way, but I'm not going to have you thinking all day I am going to stop seeing you. I love you. I want to get married. Do you still hate me?"

"No," she admitted.

"Do you still hate yourself for wanting me?"

"No."

"Are you just going to leave me hanging? Are you at least starting to love me?"

"Maybe a little," she teased him, not knowing it was possible to be this happy.

"How about, tomorrow, you close the diner early and we go pick out a ring?"

"I haven't said yes."

"You will," he teased her back.

"How do you know?" She loved bantering with him almost as much as she loved him.

"I read it in the stars."

Chapter Thirty-Six

"Can I get a refill?"

Ignoring the customer, Jody didn't remove his gaze from Sophie. Another hour, and she would be safe on the mountain.

"Excuse me. I want a refill!"

Sophie cast him a curious glance before breaking off a conversation with Lily and Rachel. Both women worked part-time at the thrift store. Rachel hadn't worked there for a while as far as he knew.

Rachel was Greer's sister, which had him wondering if she was working there by chance today, or was she working today because Greer asked her?

He had spent the day on pins and needles, waiting for what the dark star had warned them about to unfold.

"What's wrong with you today?" Sophie asked, coming up to him. "You've been acting weird all day."

"Have I? I guess my mind has been elsewhere."

Giving her sensuous smile, he laughed when she gave him an angry glare back.

"Can you get your mind out of the gutter long enough for a refill?"

"I think you might want to do that yourself."

Sophie turned in the direction of the customer. When her eyes came back to him, he gave her an innocent look.

"I'll get it," she said, lips pursed.

"I thought you might. She's drinking sweet tea."

"Of course she is."

It was everything he could do to keep a straight face as Sophie went to the drink station. He loved seeing the spark of jealousy in her each time she saw Chasity.

She had nothing to be jealous about. That man-eating bitch was one of the few single women he hadn't hooked up with. There was something manipulative about Chasity he couldn't put his finger on, and he didn't want to.

Jody watched as Sophie took Chasity her drink. After a few short words that he couldn't hear, Sophie pivoted and came back with a furious expression on her face.

"Your ex wants your opinion on what she should order."

"I don't have any exes. I had hookups."

His clarifying the situation only made Sophie angrier.

"Just go give her your opinion on what to order. Suggest something she can choke on."

Inwardly, he was still laughing when he approached Chasity's table.

"What can I get for you?"

"I was beginning to wonder if you were ignoring me."

"There aren't many men who could ignore you."

"Then why haven't you taken me up on any of my invitations to come over for dinner?"

"Chasity, when I had hookups in the past, I was very careful about the women I was with. There's one type of woman who wasn't worth the price to fuck."

"What type of woman is that?" Her flirtatious attitude turned chilly.

"A bitch like you. A frostbitten dick isn't worth the price of fucking you."

"I'll take the ticket, and I'll take my business to King's." He wrote out her ticket, and she snatched it out of his hand.

"Personally, I'd go home and cook if I were you. King's wife won't be as polite as Sophie."

The way she looked at him gave him the chills.

Sophie was waiting for Chasity at the register.

Admiring that Sophie was polite to the woman, Jody wrapped his arms around her waist.

"I'm impressed."

"By what?"

"Your restraint."

Noticing that Lily and Rachel had checked out while he was talking with Chasity, he took the opportunity to walk to the front of the restaurant and lock the door.

"We have forty-five minutes before I close." Indignantly, she started busing where Lily and Rachel had been sitting.

"By the time we get everything ready for tomorrow, it will be."

She didn't argue.

Pitching in together, they unloaded the dishes that Ginny had put in the dishwasher before she had left for the day, loaded the remaining dirty dishes, mopped, and swept. Sophie was clearing the register when the phone rang.

Jody went to lock the back door while Sophie answered the phone. He came back as Sophie slammed the phone down. His eyebrows rose at the furious way she had ended the call.

"Who was that?"

Sophie looked at him with hurt and anger. "Chasity. She told me she's pregnant."

"Why did she call *you* to tell you she's pregnant?"

"She thought I should know what kind of person you are. She said when she tried to tell you she was pregnant, you were nasty to her."

"Was she inferring *I* was the father?"

"She didn't infer anything. She came out and said so."

"Chasity is lying."

"I have no doubt she is."

Relief flooded him that she believed him ... until he saw her expression was still upset.

"You're angry at *me* because she lied about me?"

"I'm angry because I have suckered myself into thinking we could have a future together. First Baylin, and now Chastity. How many women's anger am I going to be the brunt of because you couldn't keep your dick in your pants?"

Her gradually escalating voice had him wincing.

"Do you mind lowering your voice? I don't want Greer coming over here. He'll make us heat up the grill again. Let's go home. We can talk about it—" He had to break off what he was saying when the phone rang again.

"If that's Chastity, let me talk to her," he growled as she answered the phone.

Jody could tell it wasn't Chasity when Sophie began talking in a tearful voice.

"I'll be there in fifteen minutes. Just wait," she said, hanging the phone up.

"Who was that?"

"My parents."

Reaching under the counter, she pulled her purse out.

"Go home, Jody. My parents are here. They're waiting for me at my apartment."

"I'll drive you."

Sophie shook her head at him. "No, I'm going to walk. I need to think."

"I'm not letting you walk when I can drive you."

"I'm not giving you an option. Go home. I'm going to stay the night at my apartment. There's no need coming in tomorrow, either. I won't need you."

"You're ditching me because your parents are here?"

"I'm sure you have better things to do rather than play bus boy for me. I'm not ditching you; I'm taking a break. A break where I can get my head back on straight and decide if I really want a future with you without being influenced by how good you are in bed. I just don't know how compatible we would be once we grew tired of each other."

Each word cut him deeply. While he had been falling in love with her, she was regarding their time together as sex. How many women had he told the same thing? The old saying of the shoe being on the other foot played through his mind.

"My parents are waiting." Brushing past him, she went around the counter to the door without looking at him.

She unlocked the door, and he felt the same stark emotion he could read on her face.

"Listen to me—"

"I need to hurry, Jody. Please, just go."

Hearing the crack in her voice, he went through the door, waiting for her to turn off the light and lock the door.

"At least let me drive you," he argued.

"Do I need to go to the police station to get you to leave me alone?"

Jody felt as if he had been smacked in the face. "No, you don't."

Walking around her, he went to his truck. When he got inside, he saw Sophie crossing the street. She was only a couple of blocks from her apartment building, but darkness was descending. She wouldn't make it before it turned pitch dark.

Starting the truck, he rolled the window down, watching Sophie until she turned the corner. After waiting several minutes, he pulled out of the parking lot while looking in the direction she took. Jody could see her when he stopped at the red light. She had a straight shot to her apartment building. Turning the wheels of the truck, he started to edge out of the traffic so he could keep watch over her when a breeze blew in the window, ruffling his hair.

Come home.

Silas' voice spoke to him through the wind.

Wanting to disregard his order to watch over Sophie, frustrated, he turned the wheels back in the other direction of the main road. Silas would be able to watch Sophie closer than he could unless he wanted to chance Sophie seeing him and calling the police. He was afraid that if she did, soul mate or not, he didn't know if he could forgive her. He would never harm Sophie, so her thinking she needed protection from him was like a spike through his heart.

The whole drive home was a test of wills to turn back. Silas wouldn't have called him home unless it was important. He would know, with the sighting of the blood star, he was concerned about Sophie's safety.

When he turned into the driveways, he wasn't surprised to find all of his brothers were out, watching the sky. What did shock him was the Porters being there.

Chapter Thirty-Seven

Fear dogged her footsteps the whole way to her apartment. Walking to her parents' car, she looked inside and saw it was empty. Then she heard a car door open and close.

Jerking around, she saw the man who had come to the restaurant for the money Marty owed him.

"You didn't expect me to keep them out here in the parking lot, did you?"

"Where are my parents?" she managed to get out through her fear-clogged throat.

"Safe and sound for now. You ditch the boyfriend?"

"Yes."

"Good move. Someone is waiting to blow his brains out if he shows."

"I did what you wanted."

"I want something else."

"I told you I don't have two hundred thousand dollars."

He clicked his tongue at her. "Then we're at a stonewall." The man leaned back against the car behind him.

She started crying, terrified for her parents, that Jody

might have ignored her and could show up at any minute and be killed.

"I don't even know anyone with that kind of money."

"Luckily for you, I'm willing to take something Marty was holding as a replacement."

Her eyes widened. "What? I received none of Marty's personal possessions."

"This was in the restaurant. I saw it for myself when I came in."

She stared at him in confusion.

"I want the clock hanging on the wall."

Dumbfounded, she could only stare at him. Why did he want the clock? He had kidnapped her parents for a clock?

"Get in my car. We're going to the restaurant, and you're going to bring it out to me. When I have the clock, I'll call and have your parents released, and you won't see me again. Simple, huh?"

Tell him it's not working, that it's in Jody's trailer.

A sudden breeze made her spin around, hearing Silas talking to her. Silas wasn't there, though. No one was.

Slowly turning around, she saw the man had straightened from the car and was watching her warily. Had fear made her imagine hearing Silas' voice? How was she able to hear him in her head when he wasn't there?

About to ignore the voice, she heard it again.

Trust me. Bring him here.

There was no way she was going to jeopardize the Colemans, not even for her parents' safety. She didn't believe the man in front of her was going to let any of them live.

The wind blew stronger, blowing more forcefully, and a discarded cup whipped between their feet.

We are prepared. Trust us.

It was inexplicable that she was hearing Silas' voice as if he were standing beside her. If she went with the man who had kidnapped her parents to the restaurant, they would be facing certain death, but if she did what Silas wanted her to do, they might have a chance. *If* she was really hearing Silas.

"The clock stopped working a couple of days ago. I took it to where I'm staying. Jody was going to fix it for me, but he hasn't had the time."

"You're lying!" The man's face had turned ruddy with anger.

"*No*, I wouldn't lie to you." She shook her head vehemently. "I don't want you to hurt my parents. You can stay here, and I'll go get the clock and come back."

"I'm not letting you out of my sight. You're lying about it not being in the restaurant."

"I'm not. We can go to the restaurant, and I can prove to you it isn't there."

"Fuck!"

Turning to his side, he opened his car door. The wind blew again.

Roll the window down when you're inside.

"Get inside."

Petrified, she moved to get in the car. As she started to slide inside, the man punched her in her stomach, knocking her inside the car.

She held her stomach while he slammed the car door; her lungs felt as if the wind had been knocked out of her. Gasping for breath, she was afraid she was going to pass out.

He started the car and turned toward her. "This better not be a trick. Your parents won't make it through the next hour if you're lying."

"I'm not lying," she gasped out, feeling as if her stomach was on fire. Ignoring the pain, she pressed the button to lower the window.

He immediately raised it back.

"I'm ... having ... breathing..."

He lowered the window halfway.

Raising her hand, she pointed to the exit of the parking lot. "You can go—"

"I know where I'm going. You think I haven't been keeping my eye on you? I know every move you've made since you came to town."

"Why didn't you just break into the restaurant and take the clock? You didn't have to involve me or my parents."

"You stupid bitch, the restaurant is across the street from the sheriff's office."

"All you had to do was ask me for the clock when you came to the restaurant, and I would have given it to you."

He didn't respond.

Clasping her hands together in fear, she knew from his lack of response why—he didn't want her telling anyone he had wanted something from inside the restaurant. Without saying it outright, she knew he was going to kill her.

She was clenching her hands together so hard they started to go numb.

They were still a few miles away from the turn into the Colemans' property when he turned into a parking lot.

"Why are you ...?"

He struck her across the face before she could jerk away.

"Shut the fuck up."

Holding her cheek, she watched him take out his phone.

"There's been a change of plan."

She sat in fear as he told the other person on the phone about the clock being on the Colemans' property.

"We're going to do it the same way. I'll park close to where she's staying, and she can go in and get the clock. I stopped at the bar before the Colemans' place. If I don't call you back in ten minutes, kill them."

"It will take me that long to walk to the trailer on foot. At least give me twenty minutes," she begged him, keeping her head close to the window in case he backhanded her again.

He repeated what she said in the phone. Then, after closing the phone, the man drove back onto the road.

Afraid to press her luck any further, she remained quiet the rest of the way.

Have him turn into my driveway.

"The turn is coming."

The man shot her a menacing look. "This isn't the turn you make when you come and go."

"This way is closer. I take the other turn because there is more parking there. This way is closer to where I've been staying."

"Bitch, if you're lying—"

"I'm not going to do anything that will get my parents hurt."

Panic started throbbing through her veins as he made the turn into the long driveway leading toward Silas' house.

He pulled to the side of the driveway and onto the grass when Silas' house came within view.

"Hurry, bitch, time's wasting."

She got out of the car and started running up the driveway, not knowing if she should run to Silas' house or the trailer. The problem was solved for her when she heard a pain-filled yell behind her. Spinning, she saw the man being dragged out of the car. She didn't know whether to cry in relief or be terror-stricken for her parents.

An arm went around her waist, pulling her against a warm body. Releasing a scream, she turned her head to see it was Jody. She turned around and hugged him, breaking into tears.

"Someone has my parents," she sobbed into his shoulder.

Jody's arms closed around her. "Are you hurt?"

"No."

He lifted her face to his. "He hit you." Fury filled his face.

"It doesn't hurt." Trembling, she averted her gaze when Silas and Matthew dragged the stranger past her. "Should we call the police? He said if he doesn't call whoever is keeping my parents in twenty minutes, they will be killed."

"Don't worry; we're going to make sure your parents are okay. We'll find out where they were stashed. Go inside the house. Reaper and Ginny are waiting for you."

Nodding, she forced herself to release him when his arms dropped away from her.

"Jody, he told me he would kill you if he saw me with you," she started trying to explain haltingly why she had been so mean to him. "I was trying to protect you."

"Baby, I'm not mad. I understand what you were doing. What you failed to understand is I don't need your protection."

Chapter Thirty-Eight

J ody watched as Sophie went into the house. When she
was out of sight, he hurried to where his brothers, except
Issac, had surrounded the man who had hurt his
woman. Silas and Matthew were still holding the fucker
by his arms.

Fynn moved aside so he could walk inside the circle his
brothers had made.

"Where are Sophie's parents?"

"Fuck you!" The man's face was mottled red with rage.
"They're fucking dead if you don't let me go."

Jody kept his expression impassive. "How much time do
we have, Silas?"

"Fifteen minutes."

Jody looked over at Moses, letting him know they needed
to move this along if they were going to have a chance to save
Sophie's parents. While Jody wished he could break the vow
he had made to himself about using his gift, fortunately,
Moses had no hesitation using his own gift.

Moses wasted no time removing his shirt, shoes, and socks.

"If you touch me, I'll—"

"You aren't going to be able to do shit," Jody told him, knowing what was about to come.

Readying himself, Moses raised his hands. "Let him go," he ordered Silas and Matthew.

All of his brothers took steps back as the man looked around him like a caged tiger deciding which direction to go. Before he could take a step, the ground beneath the man started to sink his feet into the softening earth.

The man's eyes started bulging out of his head in terror. "What the fuck is going on?" he shouted.

"Where are they?" Jody asked calmly.

"Fuck you!"

The man sank to his knees into the soil.

"How are you doing that? Stop it!"

Moses lowered his hands, lowering the man into the earth to his hips.

"Where are they?" Jody asked as the man struggled to pull himself out. "No?"

Moses clenched his hands into fists, taking his brother's cue. Loosening his fingers, he sank the man to his neck. Exerting his strength onto the man's throat, he unclenched his hands when Jody squatted down in front of him.

"Let me tell you what's going to happen next. Tell me where they are, or I'm going to use your head as a fucking soccer ball."

He started yelling the address out.

Jody rose to his feet as Silas called Greer to give him the address.

"Are they still alive?" Jody stared down at the man who was crying so hard snot was dribbling out of his nose.

"I think so."

Jody restrained himself from asking Moses to completely bury him before he had the information he needed. "How many are there?"

"Four."

"If you leave anyone out, you're going to be spitting worms."

Jody had no sympathy for him as they waited for Greer to call back. He looked up at the sky, seeing the blood star shining brightly.

Lowering his eyes, he kept his gaze on Silas' blank expression. Silas was concentrating on what was taking place in town. The longer Silas went without talking, the tenser Jody became. Finally, two minutes before the time would have run out for Sophie's parents, Silas spoke.

"Greer has them. Tate and Dustin are taking them to the hospital to have them checked out."

Thank Mother he wasn't going to have to tell Sophie her parents had been killed.

"Do we know who kidnapped them?"

"There were three men and one woman. Greer doesn't know who the men are—he checked them out. The woman we all know. Chasity."

When he got his hands on her, he was going to ...

"Tate had to take her out. When Dustin entered the house, Chasity took a shot at him."

"Are all the Porters okay?"

"Yes," Silas answered.

"Was anyone else shot?"

Silas raised an eyebrow. "What do you think?"

"I don't even know why I bothered to ask." Sardonically, Jody shook his head.

"What are we going to do with him?" Isaac asked, placing his foot on the top of the man's head sunk into the ground.

Silas moved to within his sight. "Why did you want the clock?"

"I don't know. I was only told to get it! Let me go!"

Silas looked at him without sympathy. "I'm afraid we can't. You could tell someone about us."

"I won't. I swear I won't!" he screamed.

Silas reached out to pat him on the head. "Don't be scared. By the time we're done with you, you'll beg us to let you die." He rose to his feet and moved away. Matthew took his spot to squat down.

He reached out his hand, and a ball of fire appeared on his fingertips. Then the smell of burning flesh filled the air.

Matthew pulled his hand back. "Why did you want the clock?"

"I don't know!"

Several more attempts were made to get the information they needed before they came to the conclusion that the man had no more information to give.

"Silas?"

Silas nodded toward the house. "Go inside, Fynn."

Fynn didn't argue.

When he heard the door close, Moses lowered his hand, and they all watched as the burned head disappeared completely under the ground.

Jody kept watching the movement of the ground until he was completely sure the man's body was where it deserved to be.

In Hell.

Chapter Thirty-Nine

Sophie wearily sat down on the bed after returning from the hospital to see her parents. Her mother was going to be kept overnight because her blood pressure was dangerously high and needed to be monitored. Her father refused to leave her side, telling her to go home and get some rest, that she could come in the morning and give him a break.

"You look wiped out."

The mattress sank next to her as Jody sat down.

Laying her head on his shoulder, she gave a shuddering sigh. "I am. I've never been so scared in my life."

His arm came around her, holding her close. "Let's take a shower and go to bed."

She just wanted to crawl in bed and pull the covers over her. However, Jody didn't give her the option, picking her up and carrying her to the bathroom.

"You bully."

Jody chuckled and pulled her glasses off. "They're crooked."

"He messed them up when he slapped me."

Jody ran his lips over her bruised cheek. "Does it feel better?"

It kind of did.

Sophie didn't put up a struggle as he removed her clothes then his before tugging her into the shower.

The warm water soothed her tense muscles as Jody washed them off.

"Are you angry with me?"

"Why would I be angry?" he asked gently.

"I could tell you were hurt by what I said. All I could think was if I did something wrong, he was going to kill you." Despite how warm the water was, she shivered. "I never believed in soul mates until I was afraid of losing you. I don't think I could bear being without you."

"You weren't going to get rid of me that easily."

Jody turned the water off, pulling her out of the shower to dry her.

"I don't want to wait. I want to marry you now."

"We'll wait."

Hurt, she put her glasses back on.

Jody grinned at her. "Oh, we're going to get married, baby, have no doubt about that fact. But I'm not going to drag you to the courthouse after you just had a terrifying experience. A week should be long enough for Ginny, Alanna, and you to plan the wedding."

After blow drying his hair, Jody went to call Silas while she did hers. Jody was still in the living room when she lay down. Leaving the light on, she closed her eyes while she waited for him to come to bed.

Half-asleep, she snuggled against him when she felt him slide in bed behind her.

"Did the sheriff get the clock?" she asked drowsily. She had given the restaurant key to the sheriff at the hospital.

"No, it wasn't there."

Her eyes flew open in the darkness.

"How is it gone?"

"Greer thinks whoever took it broke into the restaurant's back door after the man who you met in the parking lot called him."

"No one saw anyone break in?"

"No, and the clock wasn't at the house where your parents were kept."

"So, there was one more person involved who we don't know who they are?"

"That pretty much sums it up."

Sophie hesitated to ask the question she wanted the answer to but debated if she really wanted to know.

Jody's hand slipped around her waist to rub tender circles on her stomach.

"What happened to the man who drove me here?" she asked softly.

"Don't ask."

"Okay." She wasn't going to argue for an answer she didn't want to know, anyway.

His hand slipped between her thighs. "Why haven't you asked me about hearing Silas' voice at your apartment building?"

"Because I already figured it out."

"You did?"

Wiggling her hips under his exploring hand, she slid her hand until she found his shaft. "Mmhmm ... Silas must have hidden a microphone in my purse."

Jody laughed. "That's ridiculous."

"No more ridiculous than him telepathy-talking to me."

"He wasn't talking to you through telepathy."

"That's a relief. For a few seconds, I thought I was going crazy."

"You're not crazy," he assured her.

Unable to take his teasing any longer, she released his cock to roll over, then placed a thigh over his hip and buried her hand in his hair.

Before she snagged his cock back into her hand, Jody had taken the option away from her and was thrusting inside of her.

"A little warning would be nice next time," she moaned as he stroked inside of her.

Jody's mouth went to her neck, making her melt under his touch. "Why? Your pussy is wet ..."

"You can be such a man when you want to be," she complained without heat.

"Do you want me to stop?"

Her hand went to his ass, pulling him back.

"Silas isn't the only one in the family who has special gifts."

"What gifts?" she asked him absently, only half paying attention.

"Matthew can create fire, Isaac can walk in the shadows, Jacob can control water ..." Jody punctuated each revelation with a thrust of his cock.

"Sure, and I can make lightning shoot from my finger-tips," she joked, thrusting her hips toward him as her nails bit into his butt cheeks.

"None of us can do that ... yet." He groaned, rolling her over until she was on her back and he could thrust harder.

"What can you do?"

Her muscles tensed as explosions began racking her body as she came.

"I can rock your world."

Epilogue

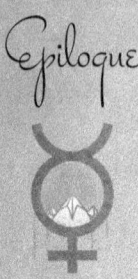

Isaac glanced out the window of the restaurant, making sure no one on the sidewalk outside was looking in. Finding no one near, he carefully stepped out of the shadows and walked directly to the wall where he took the old timey square clock down. After glancing toward the window again to make sure no one was watching, he walked back into the shadows.

Enveloped in a dim corridor, Isaac was able to move more freely without fear of prying eyes. He slowed his speed and came to a stop. Then, gathering his power, he slid the portal he wanted open to step out into Silas' living room.

Fynn and Silas followed him as he carried the clock to the dining room. He placed it down on the table, and all three of them stared at the timepiece.

Fynn reached out to touch the clock. "Why would they want this ugly piece of crap?"

Silas grabbed his wrist, moving his hand away. "I don't know."

Reaching out, Silas laid a lone hand on the clock before carefully using both hands to turn the clock over.

None of them had expected what they saw.

Glancing up, they all stared at each other, each of their faces mirroring their fear.

"Do you think they know what it is?" Isaac asked, his voice grave.

"They were willing to kill to get the clock. They knew," Silas responded grimly.

The soul mate he had been waiting for was beginning to reach his orbit. Fear nearly overwhelmed him. He would be called not only to protect the family but her as well. He was second-guessing his decision to take the clock instead of leaving it at the restaurant for Knox. He should hand the clock over to the sheriff. He had The Last Riders for protection, as well as trained deputies. He could give it to the sheriff, leaving his family and soul mate out of danger.

"What are we going to do?" Isaac looked back down at the clock then raised his eyes back to Silas.

Isaac and Fynn appeared to be just as afraid as he was.

Gingerly, he removed the golden medallion, which had been placed in a plastic bag and taped to the back of the clock. The beauty of the piece made a mockery of the cheap bag it had been placed inside of.

Silas sighed. He was weary of responsibilities. He felt as if he'd already lived a thousand lifetimes. This medallion could destroy everything his family and their ancestors had strived to achieve. They would have to use all of their gifts to protect the cherished artifact.

"Silas?" Fynn's young voice cracked in fear. "What are we going to do?"

Silas gave the answer he didn't want to give. How could the delicate piece of jewelry have the power to change the destiny of mankind? Silas couldn't explain how, only that it did. He had been groomed from birth to follow Mother. His unwavering loyalty wouldn't let him shirk the responsibility they had been given.

"We have no choice," he answered, his voice firm. "We protect it at all costs."

⁂

Jody silently slid out of bed, careful not to wake Sophie. Dressing quietly, he walked out of the bedroom to go into the other room, where he put on his shoes and a jacket before he opened the door to head out.

Striding familiarly in the direction he knew as well as the back of his hand, he made his way to the overlook where his family gathered to watch the stars. The death star was gone after destroying Chastity's star.

Kneeling, he looked up to the heaven above. "Thank you, Mother, for sparing my soul mate and her loved ones ..."

Jody stayed, giving homage to his queen until his muscles ached, only rising when he saw a shooting star racing across the sky.

Rising, he walked back to his trailer. He left the door unlocked and removed his clothes before sliding back in bed to pull Sophie into his arms.

He might be a lowly knight, but Mother had given him a king's ransom by giving him Sophie as his soul mate. A soul mate he would work hard for each day to earn the honor of calling Sophie his. She had gone to sleep still thinking he had been joking about his family's gifts; in the morning, he would have to show her the truth of his family's abilities. She had a place in their family, and he wasn't willing to keep any more secrets from her. Jody felt an overwhelming emotion as he held her in the darkness. He hadn't felt it so long that at first, he didn't recognize what the emotion was before it came to him...it was pure happiness.

Nervously, Jody shifted from one foot to the other, waiting for Sophie's reaction after witnessing his brothers' gifts.

She didn't appear happy as she watched them walking away from the trailer to return to their own homes.

Jody cleared his throat.

"I know it's a lot to accept at first."

She stared at him balefully.

"I thought you were joking last night."

"I wasn't."

"I saw that," she said sarcastically. "You don't think you could have told me before you asked me to marry you?"

"I wanted to wait until you fell in love with me. I didn't want you to be afraid of them."

Her expression gentled. "I could never be afraid of them."

She would have run in terror if she had seen them last night after she had gone in the house. Jody wisely kept that thought to himself.

"Their gifts can be inherited by their children?"

"Yes."

"Well," she gave a long, suffering sigh. "At least all I have to worry about you is passing on your good looks, which combined with my looks, at least the female population will stand a fighting chance."

Jody stared down at his nails. He needed to clip them.

"Jody?"

Should he go clip his nails now and avoid this conversation or wait...

"Jody!?"

He winced at her loud voice. "*Baby*..."

His attempt to sweet-talk her failed miserably.

"Do not *baby* me...is there something else you're not telling me? I have to go to the apartment and let the delivery drivers inside for the furniture before checking on my mom at the hospital."

"Did I tell you that Baylin moved in with her parents?"

"Yes, you did. Why are you avoiding answering my question?"

Looking up from his hands, he realized he couldn't avoid the question forever.

"Don't be mad, but I may have forgotten to mention my own gift."

Sophie narrowed her eyes on him.

"*May have*?"

He simply shrugged his shoulders. "My gift isn't as good as theirs, and you never get to see it. Whew, that's a relief off my mind. We can go now."

"Slow your roll for once, Jody!"

His shoulders slumped. "I just don't want you to overreact when I tell you."

"Do I need to go inside for me to sit down?"

"No! There are pillows in there. I prefer to talk to you out here...uh..." Realizing that he had stalled for as long as he could, he got on with it. "Have you seen the movie *The Sixth Sense*?"

Sophie moved to sit down on the trailer steps seemingly to know where this was going. "You mean the one where the kid sees dead people?"

Roughly, Jody swept a nervous hand through his hair. "Yes, well, I can see and talk to spirits who haven't been rebirthed."

"Rebirthed?"

"You might be more familiar with the term reincarnated."

She grew pale as if she herself had seen a ghost. "Oh my ..."

"Mother," he correctly interjected. "Our higher power is a woman... Mother controls the universe."

She just stared at him while Jody shifted his weight to his other foot.

"If you're ready, we can go to the hospital now to check on your mom—"

"In a minute. I need to think!"

"About what?" he asked helpfully.

"Just be quiet a second."

Jody snapped his mouth closed.

"How do you talk to them?"

This is the part he really didn't want to tell her, yet he didn't want to keep any more secrets from her.

"Two ways, they can come and talk to me if I'm in their vicinity or..."

"Or?" she asked in a strangled voice.

"Or I can call their spirts. I can force any spirit living or dead to obey me if I'm holding one of their possessions."

Sophie jerked to her feet. "Have you made me do anything I haven't wanted to do?"

Hurt, he shuttered his eyes. This was what he had been afraid of being accused of. Raising his eyelids, he stared at her honestly. "I've never used my gift to force you to do *anything*. I learnt that lesson when I convinced my dad to let us take turns on the ATV without helmets."

Jody felt her arms go around him.

"I can't even talk to them to tell them how sorry I am. They both have been rebirthed. I haven't used that ability since they died. I won't. I thought because I was on the mountain, I wouldn't have any repercussions. I didn't; they did. Silas keeps telling me Dad wouldn't have given in to me, because he had the same gift. He gave in because he wanted to."

"I agree with Silas," she said softly. "You can't blame yourself. You were only a child."

"I always will. That's why I would never use my gift to force you to do anything. I love you."

"I believe you."

She gave him a misty smile, which made him feel like Hercules.

"You may be a conceited, extremely attractive doofus, but you're mine, too. I guess I can deal with you talking to dead people as long as you don't talk to them around me or bring them home."

Jody gave her a pained expression.

"I promise... there's just a big favor I need first."

Sophie separated herself from him.

"What's the favor?" She glared at him suspiciously.

"You don't need to be here when I talk to him," Jody assured her.

"What do you need?"

"I need the letter you said Marty left you."

Sophie frowned at him.

"Why do you need the letter?"

"The letter will allow me to talk to him without being near his body. I could look for his spirit in the afterlife, but I prefer not going that route."

"Why..." Sophie broke off. "Never mind, I don't have to guess where that son of bitch is. The letter is in the drawer of the dresser. Do I need to get it for you?"

"No."

"Can I go let the delivery drivers in?"

"Go ahead. I'll meet you at the hospital."

"Okay." Sophie started to leave then hesitated. "If you talk to Marty here, can he come back here whenever he wants? I really don't want him haunting me."

"No, he can only come when I call him."

"I need a drink."

Jody heard her mutter under her breath.

"I'll chill a bottle of wine for us to drink tonight when we get home."

"Chill a case. I'm going to need several bottles." She swung back as if another thought occurred to her. "By the way, I don't need to worry about you cheating me on me with dead women, do I? 'Cause as much as I love you, that would be a deal breaker. I'm not fighting a corpse over you."

"Of course not. Don't be silly."

Deciding it was prudent, he rushed up the steps of the trailer to lock himself inside as Sophie came at him with deadly intent. Damn, he was going to have to do something about her jealously streak. The way she just looked at him, he wouldn't need the letter to get to talk to Marty; he would be his roommate in the other life.

He went into the bedroom, opened the drawer, and found a yellow envelope. Opening the envelope, he pulled out some legal papers and an unopened letter. He held it, then went outside after peeking through the window to see if Sophie was gone. Not wanting to invade her privacy, he left it unopened; it wasn't his place to read the letter before she did. He walked to the family cemetery and stood near his great-great-uncle's grave.

"Marty, father of Sophie. Come to me."

Using a voice he had never used around Sophie, he waited for the spirit he had summoned.

Nothing happened. Marty thought to refuse him. He wouldn't be denied.

"Marty, father of Sophie. I command you to come to me," he called, using a harsher tone of voice.

Marty appeared in front of him. Jody gave him time to assimilate he was no longer in Hell.

"I want answers."

Marty stopped looking around the cemetery to focus on him. His face was contorted in fear. "Why am I here?"

"I want answers."

"I don't have to tell you a fucking thing!"

Jody casually stepped forward, unafraid of the dead spirit. "I don't want to hurt you, but I will."

"You can't hurt me any more than that bastard who runs Hell."

"Believe me, I can, and I will. Don't test me."

Marty gave in. "What do you want to know?"

"Why did you leave the diner to Sophie?"

The spirit became terror stricken. "Leave Sophie alone."

Taken aback at Marty's protective instinct when he mentioned Sophie, Jody felt as if his legs had been swept out from under him. "I was under the assumption you hated Sophie."

"I love my daughter. Stay away from her!" Marty yelled at him.

"Calm yourself," Jody told him. "I'm trying to protect her, too. I need to know who from."

"Why should you care?"

"A lot's happened since you met your end, old man. I love Sophie, and I'm trying to protect her."

Marty stared at him closer. "You're one of the Colemans. I remember seeing you with them when they came to town."

"That's correct. I'm Jody. Now tell me what I need to know."

Marty seemed indecisive; his face set stubbornly.

"Ginny is my sister. She is the only one in this town who gave a damn about you. If you cared enough to get to know the rest of the Colemans, you'd know I'd only want to protect your daughter."

His face twisted in remorse.

"Ginny was the only good thing in my life, other than my daughter," Marty revealed. "I left Sophie the restaurant because it was the only thing I could. I lost all my money on the horses. The restaurant was the only thing I had to give."

Jody steeled himself not to feel sorry for him.

"If you loved her so much, then why did you leave the clock out in the open to be seen?"

"I didn't know I was going to die before they came back for the clock."

"Who was?"

"I don't know. Delormer is someone's muscle; I didn't ask. He gave me money to stash it. I did. I was in debt to my eyeballs. I wanted the money he offered more than I wanted to ask questions."

"What did Delormer look like?"

"Did?"

"If he's who I think he was, he's dead," Jody answered.

"He was an ugly fucker, looked like he had big holes on his face."

"That's him," he confirmed. "You have no idea who he worked for?"

"No. Tell Sophie to get rid of the clock."

"Why do you care? You've made her and her mother's lives miserable."

"I saved them."

Jody spat, "Bullshit."

"I'm not lying. The clock wasn't the first time I had dealings with Delormer. He was my bookie when Sophie was just a kid. I owed him money, and he threatened to kill Sophie or her mother unless I paid him back. I kept them moving until I could pay him back. I never could. He brought me the clock and told me if I kept it safe, he would cancel out the debt I owed him, plus give me fifty thousand cash. When he came back for the clock, I was going to try to make amends to Sophie... my time ran out."

"Yes, it did. Now you have Sophie tangled in the mess you created," Jody said grimly, his voice dropping to a whisper.

Marty asked frantically as his image began to disappear, "What are you going to do with the clock?"

"What you didn't have the balls to do: find out who it belongs to."

Afterword

Fate's hands clenched on the balustrade. "So, it has begun."

"It began a long time ago," Mother responded. "I told you I would fulfill my promise to you."

"I would never have wanted you to put yourself in jeopardy." Fate blinked back tears brought on by a mixture of happiness and sadness.

As always, Mother stood fearlessly firm.

"I will only be in jeopardy if they fail me. They won't."

Fate gazed over the balustrade, watching as the three humans hid the medallion. "He is afraid."

"As they all should be."

Fate returned her gaze to Mother. "What's your next move?"

Mother narrowed her gaze on all the pieces involved in the game. "There is one who has been waiting patiently for his reward. I prefer to move another piece, but my rook deserves his."

Fate frowned. "Aren't you going to lose the game if you move him too early?"

"No." Mother gave her a calculating smile. "Can you think of a better incentive to win a battle than love?"